AN UNFORTUNATE END

A LILLIE MEAD HISTORICAL MYSTERY

LISA ZUMPANO

FIELDING HOUSE PRESS

PROLOGUE

July 1919
Oxfordshire, England

ARTHUR STUART HADN'T WANTED to be a footman for a number of reasons. The first reason was that he couldn't stand the livery. The starched shirts and woollen trousers were itchy and he had sensitive skin. The spit-polished shoes he was required to wear were narrow and stiff. Arthur had the misfortune of having two wide, block-like feet, like his grandmother. They were terribly un-English feet, and more suited to a German or a Russian than to a young man from Oxfordshire.

The second reason was that Arthur's brother, Harold, had been a footman before the war and hadn't returned to his post as third footman when it ended. It wasn't that he hadn't wanted to return—he just never got the chance. Being a footman reminded Arthur of what those last, wasted years of his brother's life must have been like. Harold had wanted to be a farmer

—a sheep farmer, to be exact. But a farmer needs capital and their family had none to get him started. So instead of tending a herd, he had gone into waiting for a historied and moneyed family, who had been unappreciative and ignorant of how fine a lad he was. Arthur could imagine how defeated Harold must have felt every time a bell was rung to summon him. Day after day, night after night—the drudgery of it all. A life in service was as far away from the pastoral idyll as one could possibly get.

As far as footmen went, Arthur wasn't sure he was very well suited to the large and imposing house he resided in now. He hadn't had much experience, and, if truth be told, he was more interested in trying his hand as a salesman in his friend's wool shop on Broad Street instead. As with his brother, service wasn't Arthur's particular calling. When he had said as much to his mother, she had replied, "Hush now, lad. You are as good as anyone else they might have gotten, and a great deal smarter." She had tapped the end of his nose, the way she always did when she was finished speaking her mind, and dismissed him. *Nobody cares if a footman is smart or not*, he thought. In fact, it was an advantage to be rather dimwitted—that way, the repetition of it all was less likely to affect one's mental state.

Now, two months after he had started, he stood at the threshold of the drawing room and great hall and thought about how much he wished he had stood his ground and told his family he was taking that job in the wool shop. The late afternoon heat was stifling. A whisper of a breeze would have been a welcome relief, but there was none forthcoming. Outside, the usually lush gardens were starting to wilt. In the fields to the north, sheep grazed lazily under mammoth oak trees, their canopies a refuge from the glaring sun. It was time for a good summer rain.

Arthur watched the father and son of the house pace back and forth in the drawing room. Lord Swindon and Edgar

Swindon—intermittently alternating between sitting and standing as though no spot were restful. The drapes were drawn, shutting out the afternoon light. A housekeeper brought in pots of tea and laid sandwiches and sweets, hoping to tempt the men to eat. Arthur knew she wanted to take their minds off what was going on upstairs. But neither had an appetite, and soon flies began to buzz around the food. An attendant maid swatted at them.

The minutes ticked by painfully slowly, turning into hours. Arthur shuffled from one foot to the other, hoping his discomfort wouldn't be noticed. There was nothing to do but wait, and nothing to alleviate the waiting. Servants came and went quietly. Hushed whispers in the hallways were the only sounds, save for the ticking of the clock. An ebony Labrador retriever wandered in and out of the room from time to time, exhausted from the heat. He eventually flopped down on the stone hearth, clearly hoping the cool surface would give him some reprieve.

Arthur heard a creak on the landing and turned to see a regretful man with a stethoscope around his neck standing in the foyer, a black, weathered medical bag in his hand. Arthur wondered fleetingly how he had gotten down the stairs without him noticing. The doctor was certainly light on his feet. The men in the drawing room saw Arthur's head turn and looked up at him, as if he was about to tell them the earth-shattering news himself. But Arthur nodded and stepped back with a sweeping gesture of his hand, signalling to the men that the doctor had returned from upstairs. They quickly made their way into the foyer. Arthur settled back into his post, chin slightly raised and eyes set above the men's heads, trying to make himself invisible.

"I'm afraid I have done all I can," the doctor began quietly, shaking his head. "I haven't seen a case like this in all my time in medicine. She is declining at a rapid rate and the interventions I have employed have been futile. If it is Spanish flu, it is a strain I have never seen before. I dare say it may be something completely different. If you would allow me, sirs, I have a theory—but I stress that it is only a theory at this point. The symptoms she is showing are consistent with poisoning." He paused, clearly uncomfortable. "She is bleeding from within, and blood is now showing up in her vomit and stool. She has open sores on her back and arms that are getting worse, and she is beginning to lose her hair. I am going back to the hospital for medication to help with her comfort level and will be back within the hour. It is time to pray, gentlemen. Only God can save her now."

Both men stood speechless.

With a final apology, the doctor turned and left them. Arthur barely got to the door in time to open it for him. *Mr. Groves certainly picked a fine day to go into town*, Arthur thought resentfully. Their mistress was obviously dying and he had been left to shoulder the grief, while the butler strolled the village markets looking for God knows what.

The two men of the house looked at one another as Arthur closed the door after the doctor. Tears welled in the older man's eyes. The younger one walked forward to him and they hugged. Arthur knew they now understood their loss was imminent. The woman they loved, mother and wife, was about to be gone forever. If it really were poisoning, as the doctor suspected, this was more sinister than Arthur could have ever imagined.

He wished he were sorting bolts of the finest tartan over on Broad Street. This was the last time he would ever listen to his mother.

1

LILLIE

TWO MONTHS LATER

New York City

L ILLIE MEAD LOOKED DOWN AT her shoes. They were nothing special, nothing extraordinary. Just plain, brown shoes that should have been replaced by now. She wondered how long she had had these shoes. Five years? At least that. Since the start of the war...yes, that was it. Had it really been that long? So much had happened in five years.

These brown, nothing-special shoes had certainly seen their fair share of living. One buckle was bent, the paint peeling off of it. That had been from her friend Harry trodding on her foot as he attempted to whisk her around the dance floor to ragtime. She remembered how his clumsiness had reduced them to helpless giggles, which had quickly been stifled by an overzealous chaperone.

That was two years ago, late during the hazy summer of 1917. How she missed England. Thinking of that night now, she contemplated once again how happiness could be suddenly snatched away. How a knock on the door from a soldier in uniform could irrevocably change one's path. How the news of a man lost somewhere in the mud-soaked wasteland that was France could reduce life to something that must be endured instead of enjoyed.

Lost. What a ridiculous way to tell someone that her loved one was gone forever. *Dear, sweet Jack.* She still couldn't fathom that she would never see him again. She had looked down at her shoes that day too.

Tears blurred her vision and anguish tightened like a vice around her chest. These same very brown, very ordinary, shoes —on one sickeningly extraordinary day. She remembered how the soldier had kept talking and how his words had sounded like gibberish. There was a ringing in her head that filled up her ears and pushed his voice away. She had heard only the occasional word in a long, incessant speech that seemed as though it would never cease: *Germans, trenches, on patrol, division, onslaught.* And on it went.

After that day, Lillie's world changed. She had left England. Her flatmate Primrose had quietly helped her pack her things into two cases and accompanied her to the train station. As they waited on the platform, Primrose held Lillie's hand and told her that when someone you love dies, you either die yourself or you live. The choice was that simple. Lillie had kept her eyes focused on the horizon and willed herself not to weep. They hugged and Lillie had boarded the train, bound for port and her ship to America. She'd wondered when or if she would ever see England again.

She often thought of her friend Harry and wondered where he was and what he was doing now that the war was over. They had both loved Jack, and, although it was difficult to think anyone missed him as much as she did, she knew Harry had also suffered. She remembered sitting with Harry during their lectures at Oxford. Well, it hadn't been a real lecture for her, of course. It was a constant irritant to Lillie that women were treated as second-class citizens and allowed only to audit lectures, whereas men could gain degrees. Regardless, that had never dampened her enthusiasm for history, economics, politics or any other number of classes she could find the time to attend outside of her job at the newspaper. She missed her work there as well. As a back office editor, she had been merely a cog in a machine, but it had been rewarding work and the daily paper she had helped produce was a meaningful addition to village life.

Lillie's door opened jolting her out of her thoughts. Her sister Penny poked her head in.

"Are you coming? The guests are all arriving now." Her voice was shrill, as it often was when she felt the stress and anxiety of hosting a party. Lillie often wondered why she bothered. "*Lillie!* Your hair! You aren't even ready!" she sputtered, frustrated.

It was an ongoing annoyance to Penny that Lillie had really made no effort to adapt to Penny's and her husband Floyd's way of life while she lived under their roof. Being part of high society in New York City meant one needed to entertain properly. Penny took this very seriously—being the wife of a self-made millionaire entailed behaving correctly. It required mixing with the right people, wearing the right clothes, and serving the right food for supper. Penny and Floyd's Central Park townhouse was exactly the perfect home for the perfect couple, with wide, expansive rooms, marble inlaid floors, vaulted ceilings and an extensive house staff.

"I won't be long, I'm just...trying to get these pins...oh, darn it!" Lillie said, struggling with her hair as the long, auburn curls escaped their clasps. It was utterly hopeless. She would never look polished and she didn't care one whit.

"Oh, never mind! I will have Maria come and look after it

for you." Penny rushed out in search of her lady's maid with the determination and force of a hurricane.

Lillie stared absently at her reflection in the mirror in the meantime. Large, round, green eyes stared back at her. Her dark-brown eyebrows were naturally sharp and defined, her lashes thick and long. She had a small scar above her left eye where a neighbor's dog had bitten her when she was very young. She often rubbed it when she was anxious or contemplative, and she rubbed it now. Her reddish-brown hair was thick and shiny and a constant challenge to keep in combs. At twenty-eight years old, she was starting to notice the roundness of her face disappearing. In its place was a more chiseled nose, more defined cheeks, and an angular chin. She didn't mind the changes taking place. Truth be told, she rarely had the time or the inclination to give her appearance a second thought.

There was a tap on the door, announcing Maria. Giving Lillie a little smile, she gently started working with her hair, and within minutes had her looking infinitely more presentable. She helped Lillie into her evening gown, which was a dark, navy, sequinned chiffon over a midnight-blue, silk bodice. Penny would likely disapprove of such dark colors on an unmarried young woman. Maria had brought some diamond earrings and a white-gold-and-sapphire bracelet from Penny's jewelry case for her to wear. She stood back now and looked at her critically, her dark African eyes moving up and down as though she were evaluating a side of pork in the village market.

"Miss, the shoes?" Maria inquired, glancing down at Lillie's feet, her worn, brown shoes clearly not matching her newly adorned appearance.

"Not to worry, Maria, I wouldn't dare wear my favourite brown shoes to such an event—I should hate to have them spoiled." Lillie smiled at Maria's obvious confusion and winked. "I have some satin ones in the wardrobe, but please allow me to get them. You must go now and have your dinner—Lord knows it will be a long night. Perhaps I could sneak away later and join you in the kitchen for a game of cards before bed? Our last game left me much poorer than I would have liked."

"Miss Lillie, I don't think your sister would approve of gambling with the house staff. Certainly not on a night where she is throwing a party. Go, you will have fun, no? And perhaps you might find a handsome man to dance with?"

Lillie rolled her eyes and slumped back into her dressing chair. "Not likely, but I shall try if it makes Penny happy and frees me from her piercing stares."

Thirty minutes later, Lillie emerged reluctantly from her room and made her way down the spiral balustrade staircase to the grand foyer. A sea of coloured gowns and dark tuxedos swam before her eyes. Candlelight glinted off the polished, silver trays laden with crystal goblets of champagne and vibrant cocktails. Laughter echoed throughout the house. Women chattered and the men boomed in order to be heard above the din of the jazz quartet. She fought the immediate urge to head back upstairs to the safe confines of her room.

A quick glance into the dining room revealed an enormous table laid in fine, white linen. Down the middle of the table, purple and white flowers housed in silver bowls were laid, one after the next, on a runner of crushed, plum velvet. White-and-gold-leaf china plates were set out and flanked by a full complement of polished silver cutlery. There were at least one hundred crystal goblets. The light created prisms that danced on the backs of the velvet dining chairs, each standing at attention no more and no fewer than twelve inches from both the table and each other. In the shadows at each corner of the room, a rigid footman stood awaiting the commencement of dinner. It was a display of extravagance that even the most elite guest would appreciate.

"Lillie!" boomed a voice behind her. She turned to see

Floyd, her brother-in-law, striding towards her. He stood over six feet tall with shoulders and legs thick as tree trunks, and his immense stature always startled her. A rectangular, Nordic face was topped with a mass of thick, blond hair fashionably oiled and coiffed for the evening. His dark-blue eyes were twinkling with both humour and mischief and Lillie couldn't help but feel her usual instant affection for him.

"My dear brother-in-law. What a turnout this evening," Lillie exclaimed, feigning excitement for his sake and trying to come across more upbeat than she felt. "I haven't seen this much interest in an evening since the Mulgraves' daughter celebrated her engagement to Count Monticello. Such a scandal marrying an Italian!" She was being wry, and Floyd threw his head back and roared loud enough to stop all neighbouring conversations.

"Tell me, little one, will you give any of these young men a chance to turn the room with you this evening? I continue to fail to tempt you with any of my available friends, but perhaps this evening you might reconsider?" He raised an inquiring eyebrow. Lillie smiled, although she could feel the smile not quite reaching her eyes.

"I shall keep an open mind, as always. However I really am quite fond of being on my own, much to your and Penny's chagrin."

"I know, I know, and there isn't any pressure. Really, none whatsoever. I am just teasing you. We must all follow our own course and our own hearts, you old spinster." He smiled and pinched her cheek in a kindly way and Lillie thought, not for the first time, how lucky her sister was to have found Floyd after their parents' death four years ago. They had perished, along with ninety-seven other souls, in a train derailment near Brooklyn—an inexperienced motorman taking a corner at far too great a speed, and leaving Lillie and Penny parentless, and alone together in the world thereafter. "But come, let us go have a drink and get this evening started."

As they turned to leave the dining room, they were stopped by a tall, distinguished gentleman in his sixties wearing an Etonian school tie slightly askew. Lillie wondered why a man of his advancing years would still be wearing his school colours, and deduced he was likely not only pompous but probably grossly insecure as well.

"Good evening, Mr. Innes. Rupert Fitzherbert. We met some time ago at your club," said the stranger as he pulled a gold lighter engraved with a sailboat from his breast pocket and lit a cigarette. A plume of smoke swirled upwards and diffused the heady cloud of perfume in the room.

"Ah yes, Mr. Fitzherbert. Good of you to come this evening. Please let me introduce you to my sister-in-law, Lillie Mead."

Lillie smiled and nodded politely.

"Mr. Fitzherbert, tell us what tears you away from London and brings you to New York?" Floyd continued.

Lillie noticed the man had the open and smiling face of someone who could have been quite charming had it not been for the nervous way his watery, blue eyes darted back and forth as he spoke.

"I have a new venture I am working on. A newly discovered gemstone, would you believe it? Red as rubies and mined in the mountains of Nevada. I am here to check on the progress of the mine and arrange for a large shipment of rough crystal to be sent back to London for faceting."

"Gems, how delightful!" Floyd said. "I suggest you stay away from Penny this evening or she will have you cornered and interrogated on how she can get her hands on some."

"Ah, yes, and she should certainly have at least a bracelet or two. They really are quite fetching. And closely related to emeralds in their chemical composition—they are both part of the beryl family. We are calling them *Red* Emeralds, much to the horror of the South Americans."

"How so?" Floyd seemed genuinely interested.

"Oh, you know how these Columbians can be—they think their green beryl is the only gemstone in the world worthy of having the title 'Emerald'. Not that there is anything in a name, mind you, but it can have its advantages for marketing purposes," Fitzherbert replied, then looked inquiringly at Lillie. "Do you like gems as much as your sister does, Lillie?"

"I am afraid not, Mr. Fitzherbert. What money I have I don't wish to spend on trinkets, no matter how beautiful."

"Lillie is a writer," Floyd interjected. "An academic, really. She studies crime history, the philosophy of war, and politics— I dare say the latter encompasses the first two." He chuckled at that. "It's lucky she is naturally beautiful on top of all that, otherwise her suitors would run for the hills—a more formidable debating opponent you have never encountered."

"Yes, quite," Mr. Fitzherbert answered, glancing distractedly around the room.

By this time Lillie had had quite enough of idle chit chat about jewels and decided to get that drink. She excused herself and made her way across the drawing room. Spotting Penny talking to a group of three ladies, each one more elaborately dressed than the last, she strode purposefully past them toward the bar, hoping not to be drawn into their conversation.

"Gin rickey, please," she requested from the bartender, who raised an eyebrow at a lady ordering for herself. He was a new face in the house, she noticed. He must have been hired for the evening.

"Yes, miss." The server mixed the drink and handed it to her with a slight bow. "Are you enjoying yourself this evening?"

"Not particularly, if you must know," Lillie replied, taking a rather unladylike extended sip of her drink. "Delightfully delicious, thank you. I am enjoying myself a little more now." She smiled at him and made her way to a chair by the large, stone hearth in the hopes of avoiding further conversation. Here she could see out the tall, leaded windows to the opalescent, brightly lit street below. Across from it was the vast darkness of Central Park. On clear days she would beg a riding horse from her sister's stable and explore the park on horseback, trotting along the clay track for a mile or so before picking up a controlled canter and going for miles, just the sound of hooves and wind in her ears and the soft squeak of rubbing leather on the saddle.

When she had been in England during the war, she had loved being social. She had especially enjoyed her time at the local pub with her roommate Primrose. From her work as a governess, Primrose had no shortage of hilarious daily stories about her little charges and the naughtiness they could get up to. When Harry was home on leave from his job in London at the War Office, the three of them would while away the evening hours laughing and carrying on as though they were able to temporarily escape the horrific war that was going on. Her favourite gatherings were, of course, when Jack could be with them. The four of them would spend their days off rowing down the Thames to a riverside pub for a lazy lunch and far too much ale.

It had been unfortunate when Primrose had fallen hopelessly in love with the handsome middle-aged widower she was working for at the time. They all knew it would come to nothing but heartache, and so it did, but Harry had been the most affected by the loss of Primrose's company. Lillie knew, even if Harry didn't, that his feelings for Primrose ran far deeper than mere friendship.

How she missed them all. She often wondered why she had run off back to New York when so much of her heart and soul was left in England. Although she was an American, England was home, thanks to her late father who had conducted much of his business across the Atlantic. But what would an England without Jack look like? She quickly stopped her thoughts from spiralling downwards. She mustn't give in to the dark depths of despair again. Instead, with another gulp of gin, she shoved away all her feelings of sadness and returned her attention to the gathering.

She noticed Floyd was still deep in conversation with Mr. Fitzherbert and for some reason she found this disconcerting— the man made her uneasy. She wondered what he could possibly be saying that had her brother-in-law so entranced. Then, out of the corner of her eye, she noticed a friend of Floyd's circling the room, his focus on her. Inwardly she groaned. He was a pleasant enough fellow, but she found him to be like a leech on a rock, clinging hopefully to something that was never going to give it sustenance.

"Hello, Lillie," he said, smiling in a way that resembled a leer, his teeth crooked and yellowing. A bead of sweat was forming above his brow and his thinning, ash-brown hair had seen too much pomade. The result was an oily slick.

"Hello," she replied vaguely, having forgotten his name entirely.

"It's Warren Hobster," he reminded her.

"Yes, of course, Mr. Hobster. Lovely you could make it this evening." She paid him the customary lip service in a clipped tone, hoping to dissuade him from staying long.

"It is a delightful gathering as usual. Floyd insisted I come, even though I am so very busy at the bank and I find most of my nights I am dining at my desk with a sandwich on my blotter and a cup of tea balanced on my lap."

"You must be very enthusiastic about your work, Mr. Hobster." The conversation had already gone on longer than she would have liked.

"Yes, indeed I am. And as I have no wife I have no restraints on my professional life."

Here it goes, Lillie thought. If she didn't excuse herself quickly, she might never get away.

"Yes indeed, I understand..." she said, trailing off and glancing around the room. "Ah, is that Mr. and Mrs. Williamson? Please excuse me, Mr. Hobster—I have been searching for them all evening!" With that Lillie dashed out of her chair and into the other room in search of someone, anyone at all, to validate her excuse.

Really, of all things. Did Floyd expect her to take up with Mr. Hobster? Is that why the trying gentleman was here tonight? Honestly, she would never get a moment's peace until she was married off. She supposed that at her age she was already a spinster in the eyes of her sister, but the war had made many widows so it was hardly unusual to see a woman alone in the world these days.

Dinner was announced and the guests made their way to the dining room. Penny had painstakingly written, reviewed, and then re-reviewed the six-course menu. A salmon mousse was the starter, followed by a Waldorf salad and crab-stuffed mushroom caps. For dinner, the cook had prepared a spiced ham with mashed potatoes and asparagus tips au gratin. Dessert was Venetian vanilla ice cream and assorted cakes with coffee and tea. Lillie knew the cook had been slaving away in the kitchen for days because she had been noticeably absent at the last two card games. Apparently it had been worth the effort on her part. Everything was delicious and many of the guests commented to that effect, making Penny positively beam.

The dinner did more to make Lillie happy than the company at the table did. Stuck between Mr. Hobster and a woman whose voluminous skirts were desperately in need of a second chair to house them, Lillie found the dinner long, hot, and terribly boring.

On the other side of Mr. Hobster sat Mr. Fitzherbert. From

time to time she noticed them speaking to each other in hushed tones and wondered how they knew each other. Mr. Hobster looked uncomfortable and anxious with whatever the content of the conversation was. Lillie heard only snippets of what they were saying over the din of clinking silverware and other diners' conversations, although it appeared to be scientific in nature. She overheard Mr. Hobster say the name Curie, and tried to recall where she had heard it before. She eventually gave up eavesdropping and focused instead on finishing her supper as quickly as possible.

She was relieved when the guests broke after dinner and a dance floor was cleared in the foyer. The jazz band provided the perfect cover for Lillie to sneak away. She did one lap around the room so Penny could see her socializing with the guests, then exited quietly through a hidden door off the foyer that led to a servants' staircase. She half hesitated on the sparse landing behind the door, wondering if she should go down to the kitchen and try to salvage a card game with the few remaining staff who weren't running around attending to the guests. In the end, she decided she was really too tired to count aces and headed up the stairwell instead.

Back in her room away from the noise and the guests, Lillie removed her shoes and dress and pulled on a silk robe. She pushed back the drapes and opened the window to get some fresh air. At her dressing table she removed the pins from her hair and let it fall down her back while she rubbed cream onto her face to remove the rouge and lipstick Maria had helped her apply. She felt as though she were removing a costume. She stood and walked to the window to gaze at the September stars. The crisp air smelled of impending autumn: wood smoke mixed with damp grass. She pulled back her bed covers and switched off the light.

In the darkness of the room she could see the street below, empty at this late hour, the occasional car puttering by. She noticed a figure step out of the shadows and stare up at her window.

How odd.

In the darkness of the room she felt sure the person couldn't see her, but she could clearly see him. She remained very still while she watched him.

He stood motionless.

She began to feel uncomfortable and wondered if he actually could see her. What was he doing? Why would someone at this time of night be outside staring up at her window, especially while there was a party going on downstairs? Surely those windows offered much more exciting views. He was wearing a dark hat and an overcoat with the collar pulled up around his neck. She could see his breath against the cool night air.

He remained there for a minute or so, absolutely still. Then he turned slowly on his heel and walked back into the shadows.

2

HARRY

A FEW HOURS LATER ACROSS THE Atlantic, Harry Green leaned over the white rails at Newbury Racecourse and watched his young thoroughbred complete the morning training session. As the huge, chestnut horse thundered by on the grass track, his exercise rider tipped his cap at Harry and gave him a huge grin. *They must be faster today.* He watched the back side of the animal as his rider brought him down to a trot and then an eventual walk, letting the reins slacken and allowing the horse to stretch his head down.

Harry pulled the flaps of his hat down around his ears and adjusted his wool scarf. The sun was barely up and the air had a chill to it. It promised to be a perfect fall day, with clear crisp skies and trees lit with coloured leaves that stretched far as the eye could see. If it weren't for his damn headache he might actually be enjoying himself.

Although a headache was probably the least he deserved after a late night drinking entirely too much whiskey and trying, unsuccessfully, to win one last snooker game in the smoke-filled village pub. He watched a group of horses in the distance make their way from the stables to the track, listening to the chit chat of the riders as their jumpy mounts tossed their heads and snorted. *Who on earth would have the guts to actually get on one of those animals?* he wondered.

He started toward the stable block to talk to his rider, when he saw a young man in the distance making his way over to the rail. Harry hesitated. The man looked familiar, and as he got closer Harry recognized him.

"Edgar!" he called, waving him over to where he stood. An old friend from school was certainly a welcome addition to a morning at the track.

Edgar had aged since their college days. He had always been tall, but was thinner than when Harry had last seen him, and now his face looked drawn and gaunt. His thick, ebony hair was longer than Harry remembered and curled where it met the collar of the heavy tweed coat he wore. His dark eyes were hollowed. Although still handsome, he looked measurably different. Edgar had always been a serious fellow and had never gotten up to the shenanigans that Harry had in school, but they'd been friendly with one another and played together on the Oxford cricket team. Harry had recently read about the death of his mother, Lady Eleanor Swindon. Her obituary had surprised him—she was only fifty-two, and was always active and healthy. Harry shook his hand warmly.

"Harry, old chap." Edgar seemed genuinely pleased to see him.

"Edgar. How long has it been? I was terribly sorry to hear about your mother."

"Thank you. Yes, it came as quite a shock. It is hard to believe she has been gone for two months," he said, growing dim. "I don't know if my father will ever recover from her death. I had to come out today—I couldn't stand another minute in that sad house."

"Ghastly, this Spanish flu. Absolutely pandemic."

Edgar looked thoughtful for a moment, as though he were trying to find the right words. They watched a couple of horses canter by, their riders chatting as though they were simply having a whiskey together. Their voices echoed above the sound of hooves.

"Harry," Edgar said finally. "I don't think it was the flu. I don't talk much of this, but my father and I were told by the doctor that he thinks mother was poisoned."

"Poisoned! My God. How on earth...?"

"Exactly, how—and why? That is the big question. A post-mortem report showed signs consistent with poisoning. We called in the police to investigate but, well, to be honest, they weren't very helpful. They did a preliminary investigation, but nothing came of it."

"I don't know how helpful the Constabulary is, truthfully. England is certainly a changed country since the war. You aren't the first member of the upper class whose experience with law enforcement lately has been less than satisfactory. We are rapidly becoming a species of dwindling importance in the eyes of this country."

"Indeed. That is my father's sentiment as well. But what is to be done now? She is dead and buried, and we must all find a way to carry on."

"Sirs?" The two men started at the voice of Harry's manservant behind them. "Tea is served by the car, if you would care to follow me."

They turned to see Rumple standing at attention, the picture of English service: middle aged with military-style iron grey hair and clothed in, of all things, a woollen navy and emerald kilt, charcoal-coloured lambswool socks, ghillie brogues, and a dark tweed blazer.

"Ah, Rumple, always sneaking up on me. I shall have a heart attack one of these days. Could you not give a warning before you spring yourself on us?" Harry admonished in mock jest. He raised an eyebrow at his clothing. "I say, are your feet not wet in those shoes? The grass is terribly damp this morning. And what on earth has taken you so long to lay the tea? Not at the betting again, are you?" Rumple stood stone faced, eyes set on the horizon. He'd lost a small fortune the last time Harry had brought him to the track.

"Edgar, come, let's have something warm. Rumple, did Rose pack any of those tasty little lemon cakes I asked for?"

"She did, sir."

"Delicious. Just delicious. Edgar, you must try one. Rose is a wonderful cook, her tea sweets are to die for," Harry announced loudly over his shoulder as they walked off, intending Rumple to hear him. He had lately noticed a blossoming romance between his manservant and his cook, and wisely deduced that making his usual jokes about her food in front of Rumple was a thing of the past.

He whispered to Edgar, "Just don't come for dinner, her roasts are tougher than snakeskin."

Edgar smiled and followed Harry to a very large and immaculately polished Rolls Royce Silver Ghost. Beside the automobile, Rumple had erected a small wooden table with a dark yellow and black tartan tablecloth. Set upon it was an early nineteenth-century silver tea set handed down from Harry's grandmother, each piece polished to perfection. The set, designed by Gorham Silver, had been brought back from America by his late grandfather. The family had often joked that America was making better silver than the Europeans. The delicate, white, bone-china cups and saucers, rimmed in ebony, provided a perfect complement to the tea set. Rumple had ensured there was plenty of cold milk in the creamer, enough sugar lumps to delight twenty children, and a colourful assortment of fairy cakes and tarts.

He deftly opened another wooden folding chair for Edgar and slung two thick oatmeal-coloured woollen blankets over their backs to keep the men warm while they took their tea and watched the horses. Harry and Edgar settled in while Rumple busied himself pouring tea and arranging baskets by the boot of the car.

"Have you a horse here this morning?" Harry asked.

"Father and I do, yes. A few, in fact. He has all but lost interest in them since mother's death, but I like to watch them go. I am looking forward to the Stakes this Sunday. And you?"

"Just one, yes. Attila. A big chestnut. Irish bred."

"Interesting choice of name, given what we have just gone through with the Germans."

"Mmm, hadn't really thought of it that way," Harry replied, reaching for a slice of lemon cake. "But he *was* a fierce warrior. Hard to believe where we sit now was a German internment camp during the war. Did you ever see it?"

"I was stationed here briefly in '14 with the East Lancashire Regiment. It was taken over by the reservists shortly after and we moved on. Terribly depressing. Row upon row of tents, corrugated metal fencing, miserable, confused people. Glad to have it over with, I can tell you." Edgar sipped his tea thoughtfully. "Ah, here comes one of ours now, have a look."

A beautiful, delicate, ink-black horse came around the bend and settled in at a comfortable gallop along the straight away in front of their table. Harry thought he could see a trail of long dark hair from under the rider's cap.

"Is that...I say...who is your rider, Edgar?"

"I can't get a thing past you, can I, old sport? Father and I feel the finer, more sensitive horses do better with female riders."

"And you think *I* am controversial!" Harry retorted. "I don't suppose they let her in the jockeys' dressing room."

"She doesn't mind. As long as she is beating them, she seems to be quite content."

The two of them sat in companionable silence while they

watched the riders and horses. After a few minutes, Harry said, "Listen, if I can do anything to help with finding out the truth behind your mother's death, please don't hesitate to ask."

Edgar sighed. "I have been trying to come to peace with it— but I can't without knowing who is responsible and why they would have done such a thing. If we knew the truth, I think Father might be able to begin healing."

"I do have an idea of where to start shaking the trees," Harry mused, a plan formulating in his mind that had implications beyond Lady Swindon's death. A bird and two stones came to mind.

"Tell me."

"You say the police have been most unhelpful. I agree law enforcement for our kind has been lacklustre to say the least—I wouldn't be surprised if we have a Labour government before long. Such a changing world. Having said that, there is nothing more annoying to the Oxfordshire Constabulary than a discussion of their incompetence in the press. It is sure to draw attention, not only from the public, but also from Scotland Yard. No local police force wants to look like a bunch of ninnies in the eyes of the Yard."

"Are you suggesting having a story published in a newspaper?"

"Precisely. And the sooner the better."

"Which paper would oblige us?"

"I know someone over at the Oxford Daily Press, head of the news division. A bit of a wurp but I can usually get what I need from him. Leave it with me. I will be in touch with you once I know the timing. Now, have some more tea and tell me where I can find your girl jockey. I like her style."

LATER THAT AFTERNOON Harry emerged from his dressing room

back at Tynesmore followed by his enormous, mottled grey Irish wolfhound. The two of them wandered into the yellow silk-walled dining room in search of a light lunch. With some relief and a rumbling stomach, Harry was pleased to see Rumple had arranged to have the sideboard laid with a series of warming plates, a basket of bread, a cheese board, and a large bowl of fruit. Harry helped himself to some warm sausages and roasted potatoes and popped an apple in his pocket. As an afterthought he added a few slices of cheese.

"For you, Constance," he said, patting the great hound gently on her head. "Not too many, as I don't want you getting sick in the car. There's a good girl."

He sat at the head of the table, feeling ridiculous, as he always did when he was in the dining room alone. He really must get rid of this absurdly gigantic table and replace it with something more befitting of a bachelor. With his brother gone to Switzerland for the foreseeable future and his parents abandoning country life for the glitz and glamour of their London townhouse, it appeared Harry was a man adrift on a rambling estate in Oxfordshire.

Lucky for him, Tynesmore was a respectable house but not an exceedingly large one. He was able to get by quite happily with Rumple, a cook, and a housekeeper. If they needed extra manpower, they only had to look as far as the local village for temporary labour. Although the grounds belonging to Tynesmore were extensive, Harry had long ago given up the facade of maintaining traditional English gardens in favour of letting the horses have the run of the place. Fields were fenced and cross fenced for pasture grazing, and at the end of the war Harry had extended the gallops to circle the entire estate so most of the horses' training could be done on site. The stable block was manned by an eccentric old Scotsman who had a myriad of young lads mucking and feeding the Greens' arsenal of horses at all hours of the day.

Harry sat in the silence of the room and quickly wolfed down his lunch as Constance, lying at his feet, did the same with her cheese. He rang for Rumple, who emerged a few minutes later, immaculately dressed in tall polished black boots, a double-breasted olive-green chauffeur's coat, and a black cap.

"Honestly, Rumple, nothing gets by you, does it. How did you know I wanted to go for a car ride?"

"I heard you mention to the young Lord Swindon that you wanted to discuss something at the newspaper and I anticipated your wanting to go into town."

Harry frowned at him. "I notice you call Edgar 'Lord', however, you do not afford me the same title."

"You said once the use of titles is archaic in a new and modern England."

"Rumple, may I remind you my father is Earl Egglington? And when I told you that, I was intoxicated and trying to relate to the chaps around the card table."

"Yes, sir."

Harry studied Rumple for a moment. While his servant was at least forty, he remained fit and youthful. His gray hair, rather than detracting from his appearance, gave him an air of authority. Rumple had been too old to go to the front during the war and had instead done various tasks for the government under the guidance of the Defence of the Realm. The little he knew of Rumple's wartime duties was not only a result of the manservant's discretion, but also because of the culture of secrecy that shrouded the department. Harry supposed that serving one's government was hardly the same as serving a man of Harry's own age and rank and concluded that he was lucky to have his loyal manservant and friend. Their current discussion was hardly important and Harry didn't want to irritate Rumple unnecessarily. He opted for the path of least resistance.

"Good, I am glad that is settled. Shall we go? Would you mind bringing the car around?"

"Yes, *my Lord*, right away." Harry thought he could detect the slightest sarcasm in Rumple's tone. He chose to ignore it. Good help wasn't easy to find these days.

THE OFFICES of the Oxford Daily Press were located on Cornmarket Street. Rumple pulled the Rolls Royce up to the curb in front of the building and leapt out of the car to get Harry's door. Harry walked up the limestone steps to a glass front door, subtly checked his appearance in its reflection, and, satisfied, entered the lobby. Beyond the reception desk an industrious newsroom whirred with clacking typewriters, animated conversation, and the dull overhead roar of the second floor printing presses.

Rumple stepped up to the front counter, jutted out his chin and announced ridiculously loudly over the din, "A Mr. Harry Green to see Mr. Jeremy Winston."

The effect of his booming voice was instant. The secretary quickly busied herself with locating her boss as Harry gave Rumple a wink and a triumphant smile. If Rumple noticed, he certainly didn't let on, and continued to stand at attention.

A few moments later, a thin and wiry middle-aged man clad in a cheap, brown suit and day-old facial hair entered the lobby and shook Harry's hand.

"Harry, it's been a long time. Come into my office."

"Jeremy, thank you for taking the time to see me."

The two men wandered through the newsroom to a small, stuffy office at the rear of the building. Closing the door behind them, Jeremy circled a desk piled high with papers and dirty teacups and took his seat. "So tell me, what brings you to my humble newspaper?"

"I will get straight to it," Harry said, flopping into a worn leather armchair. "Have you heard of the death of Lady Eleanor Swindon?"

"I did, yes. Flu, wasn't it?"

"Apparently not. The attending doctor thinks she was poisoned."

"Police investigate?" Jeremy picked up a pencil and chewed on the end of it.

"To some extent, yes, but they were uninterested and sloppy. They didn't pursue any leads, or even look for leads for that matter. I think there is more to this than meets the eye. I want your paper to write a story on the incompetence of the Constabulary. But more than that, I want you to have one of your crime reporters investigate. Think of the headline: 'Oxford Daily Crime Reporter Discovers What Police Failed to Notice.' That sort of bent. Why not?"

"I can point out many reasons why not," Jeremy retorted. "I have only one crime reporter employed on staff, and he is overworked as it is. Everyone else is busy reporting on big issues: unemployment, the plight of the returning war hero, housing shortages, alcoholism, moral decay, the list goes on and on. I just haven't the manpower to help you out. Not only that, this could be a dead end, no pun intended. The doctor could have been mistaken. There could be no story and it could end up being a big waste of time."

"Jeremy, I am disappointed in you. You are a news man, and there is a possible murder, of a Lady no less, on your very doorstep. Surely this sleepy village would be interested to hear of a *murder*. Shall I walk this down the street to another newspaper then, give them the leg up?"

Jeremy looked pensive. Harry knew he wanted it, but the wheels were turning on how to make it all happen.

"I'll tell you what," Harry continued after a precisely timed moment, pleased the conversation was playing out just as he'd planned. "Why don't I get you another reporter? I will pay the initial time to get her up to speed—it can be her training period, if you like. And after that, she will be employed by your paper to report on this case. Once all is said and done, if you don't need her anymore, she moves on."

"*Her?*" Jeremy queried.

"Yes, you remember Lillie Mead. Worked for you in editing a few years back."

"You want me to put a woman on crime reporting? You must be joking."

"I never joke—well, almost never—and certainly not now. And she isn't just a *woman*. She is educated, brave, and can write the pants off most of the staff you have here. She can flesh things out, get the police to pay attention to this case. What have you got to lose?"

"All right, all right. You are wearing me down. Have her come in and see me tomorrow and I will see where we are at. But no promises."

"Might take a few more days than that, old chap. She is in America. But don't despair, I'll get her to this side of the pond— and right quick."

3

LILLIE

IF THE WIND WERE BLOWING JUST right off the Hudson river, New York mornings would sometimes smell of freshly baked bread and strong coffee. The air would breathe in from the West, gather steam over the rooftop of Sol's Deli, and deliver its delicate scent through the gauzy drapes of Lillie's bedroom. That was if she had the foresight to sleep with her windows open, as she often did.

This morning, Lillie stretched and threw back her bed covers, inhaling deeply, feeling the cool air on her skin. Shivering, she hurried to dress, both for warmth and because she wanted to get to the stables before the rest of the house rose. Although the morning after a party should ensure that everyone had a little lie in—the band had gone until at least one o'clock in the morning—Floyd often had difficulty sleeping and would take to drinking excessive cups of coffee in his mahogany office, the floor littered with the daily papers, long before the first pink light rose over the Manhattan skyline.

She crept down the stairs and through a foyer still littered with champagne flutes, grabbed her boots and a quilted riding coat from the hallway closet, and exited the house through the back door. In contrast to the house, the stables were a flurry of activity. The horses were already eating and an army of stable lads were coming and going. She watched as two of her favourite riding horses were led out of the building, their thick tails swishing, and handed off to a couple of men she didn't recognize who were standing in the cobblestone driveway. She hustled after the horses and introduced herself to the two new faces.

"Are you taking the horses somewhere? It seems very early..."

The groom looked startled to see her. He shuffled his feet nervously and fiddled with the end of the lead rope, fingering the leather flick as he spoke. "Oh, Miss Mead, uh, I thought your sister would have told you."

"Told me what?"

"The horses have been sold. These two gentleman are picking them up."

"Sold? I don't understand. Which horses? Just these two?"

"No ma'am, all of them."

How could that be? *All* of them? Neither Penny or Floyd had mentioned a thing. She was astonished. Spinning on her heel, she walked quickly back to the house. She flung open the back door and took the stairs to her sister's bedroom two at a time.

"Penny!" She tried to calm her voice but found its agitated tone indelible. Her older sister was awake, sitting up in bed with a tray on her lap and a look of trepidation on her face. "Did you know all the horses had been sold?" Penny nodded but, unusually for her, remained silent. "But why didn't you tell me? Why would you sell them?"

Penny patted the bed, motioning for Lillie to join her.

"We had to. Floyd has had some...how should I put it...some financial issues as of late. Nothing to worry about, he assures me, but his capital is tied up in things that he can't sell, so cash is a bit tight, just for now. He says he will buy everything back as soon as he can."

"What is 'everything'"? Are there more things, beyond the horses, that are gone?"

"A few of the antiques, nothing we would really miss, and some of my jewelry. But it doesn't matter—I have so much of it anyway." Her face displayed a false brightness. She tried to raise her teacup to her lips, but it rattled dangerously, so she set it back down on the tray instead.

"But you threw that huge party last night, and all the food, and staff, and champagne—it must have cost a fortune."

"It had been planned so long in advance, and Floyd didn't want to cancel it. The appearance of that would have been...well, demoralizing really. And it won't be for long, you'll see. Floyd has a wonderful knack for making money." She motioned to the grand bedroom and gave her a vacant smile. Lillie felt instantly sorry for her.

She lowered her voice. "What about your fortune—the money Father left us...has Floyd appropriated that as well?"

Penny reluctantly raised her eyes. "A great deal of it, yes. But he doesn't know about my account in Switzerland, I have kept that private. And anyway, everything will be back to normal very soon." She patted her hand, and silence weighed in the air. After a minute, she said, "I am sorry about the horses, I know how much you loved them...I didn't know how to tell you. I wanted to, I tried..."

Lillie, thankful their parents had the foresight to split their inheritance and place some of it in an off-shore account, smiled at her sister, shaking her head to silence her. The horses could be bought back. It was Penny's confidence, something Lillie had rarely seen waver, that would be harder to recover.

4

September 2, 1919

Dearest Lillie,

Constance and I have missed you terribly. Terribly! It is my hope that by the time you receive this letter you have already been contacted by a representative of Cunard Shipping Lines. The ticket they are providing, departing New York on October 11, is a first class passage to England. Non refundable, I might add. I don't want even a whisper of resistance from you now that I have spent the equivalent of Rumple's annual salary on your ticket.

The long and the short of it is, I need your help. Well, actually a friend of mine needs your help. I will explain all when you arrive but suffice it to say it is a life and death situation.

It has been two long years since you left and I know you are infinitely unhappy trouncing around New York as a socialite. Not really your style, my dear. It is high time you escape all those American suitors and return to the fold. I need you here! I am having a terrible time disciplining Constance and Rumple is becoming more eccentric by the day. Moreover, I really cannot decide which wall covering I should choose for the drawing room. This may sound frivolous but I assure you it is not. Imagine I choose poorly and am subjected to ridicule from all the other dukes, lords and earls of Oxfordshire, or even worse, their wives—to say nothing of their mistresses.

I will be there to greet your ship when it arrives. Rest assured if you choose to return to New York after our little job is completed I shall respect, begrudgingly, your decision. Of course I hope you stay forever, my darling girl.

With greatest affection,

Harry

~

SEPTEMBER 12, 1919

DEAR HARRY,

I appreciate your sentiments and I am flattered that you think I may be of any help with your choosing a suitable wall covering. As for the 'life and death situation' you refer to, while I am sympathetic to whatever you may have poked your nose into this time, I really cannot come back to England. I have a very active life here in New York and, if you must know, England holds sad memories that I am unwilling to face. Call me a coward, but there you have it.

I do miss you though, very much, and I miss Primrose. Incidentally, do you ever see her? I always thought the two of you would have made a capital match, but I suppose your family has other plans for their youngest son.

All my love,

Lillie

~

SEPTEMBER 22, 1919

LILLIE,

I cannot even begin to imagine when you became so stubborn! I need you here! Immediately! Please do not delay. If you must know, a friend of mine's mother has been murdered. Jeremy Winston from the newspaper wants to hire you as his crime reporter. This is surely far more important than whatever dress fitting you might be attending this week. If I need to sail the Atlantic Ocean to come and retrieve you, I will.

On the subject of sadness...my dear, whether you are in England or America the fact remains the same. Jack is dead. We all loved him, but I know you loved him with all your being. Sometimes, our greatest fear—that of our grief—needs to be faced head on and in the company of friends. War has certainly taught us many lessons, but moving forward in life in the face of tragedy is the greatest lesson of all.

Please come. I assure you whatever pain you feel now will not be any worse here. I can't do this without you.

Affectionately,

Harry

~

SEPTEMBER 30, 1919

HARRY,

Please don't bully me. I can't possibly come to England at

the drop of a hat. I am terribly sorry to hear about your friend's mother. And murdered no less! What a shame. I wish you luck finding her killer.

Lillie.

～

TELEGRAM

October 10th, 1919

If you do not get on that ship tomorrow I am sending Rumple...STOP

I mean it...STOP

When a friend calls you must answer...STOP

I promise you will survive...STOP

5

I T WAS A SHARP AND CLEAR OCTOBER morning when a man in a dark overcoat emerged from the brick building on Melbury Road in central London and quickly made his way towards the train station. His trip to Southampton would give him ample opportunity to review the files in his briefcase and play catch up after his time abroad.

It was silly to make the trip today. His schedule was absolutely full, with not the slightest bit of time to detour off course, but some things were necessary in order to put his mind at ease. His training had been thorough and he was very aware he was breaking the rules. An old friend of his would have said *rules are made to be broken,* and he smiled to think of him now. It seemed like an eternity since he saw him last.

The station was teeming with travellers, but he easily found his platform. He had been in so many train stations all over the world that by now it was all second nature to him. Boarding the train, he found his seat and settled in for the journey. Instead of the customary removing of his hat, he pulled the brim lower over his eyes and took a leather-bound folder out of his briefcase. Inside was a stack of research papers that would take the majority of the journey to review. As the train pulled out of the station he looked up and was relieved his compartment had only a few occupants: an elderly man whose hands shook as he tried to unlatch his bag and retrieve a book and a young woman who wore bright-red lipstick and a small, salmon-coloured felt hat. He looked away as she tried to catch his eye.

The buildings thinned out as the train gathered speed and left London behind, giving way to rolling fields and farmland. As they made their way southeast, the train's journey was punctuated from time to time by stops at small villages.

The time seemed to pass slowly. Although he had intended to read the documents he carried in their entirety, he was distracted and anxious, his mind wandering. He found himself forgetting what he had just read and having to reread his pages. He eventually gave up and surrendered to staring out the window.

Finally they arrived in Southampton and the man made his way from the station to the port. In the dock was the majestic RMS Alexandria. Four smoke stacks loomed precipitously over the cabin deck and onboard there was a flurry of activity as the crew prepared passengers for disembarking.

He was used to gliding, unseen, in and out of situations, moving amongst crowds of people, murmuring salutations without ever being remembered. Once he had even attended a small formal gathering at the Winter Palace with not more than fifteen people and even then, in that heightened sense of anxiety and security, he had seamlessly negotiated the troubled waters of diplomacy and observed, participated in and executed the perfect operation—all the while not drawing the least bit of attention to himself.

Today he found an inconspicuous place to stand among the waiting crowd where he could see the gangway passengers leaving the ship. He bought a newspaper from a porter and held it in front of his chest for a potential cover. Half an hour passed as he watched passenger after passenger arrive, causing joyful reunion after joyful reunion. He couldn't help but be moved by the power of human connection—something he missed.

At last he saw her. She looked tired as she made her way off the ship, a porter trailing behind her carrying two large suitcases. Her hair seemed darker, her face and body thinner. She wore a deep wine-coloured suit and a dark, grey hat. On her feet were a pair of brown shoes that matched a large dark shoulder bag she carried.

She spotted someone on the opposite side of the crowd from where he stood, and waved. Within seconds, an enormous grey dog burst out from the crowd of onlookers and almost bowled her over in its excitement. Far from being startled, she dropped her bag on the ground, almost tripping her porter, and threw her arms around the dog as it enthusiastically licked her face.

A moment later an impeccably dressed, flaxen haired man made his way through the crowd and gathered her in an enormous embrace, lifting her feet off the ground. The dog barked hysterically, jumping around them, leash trailing. Putting her down, the man picked up the end of the leash and relieved her of her shoulder bag. He took hold of her hand and pushed his way through the crowd to a waiting car. The three of them were soon swallowed up by a sea of people.

Satisfied, the man turned on his heel and made his way back the way he came, flipping up the collar of his overcoat as he walked.

6

LILLIE

L ATE THAT EVENING IN THE comfortable library at Tynesmore, Lillie sank, exhausted, into an overstuffed armchair beside a roaring fire. Following their enormous dinner in the dining room, Rumple had left them with two large brandies and retired to his quarters for the night. Harry fussed with the gramophone as Lillie struggled to keep her eyes open.

"Aha," he exclaimed. "This is delightful, you will love it. It's a blues song called Dardanella. One of my favourites, it just came out this year."

As the music began to play softly, Lillie thought guiltily, not for the first time since her ship had docked earlier that day, how pleasant it was to be back in England and away from the troubles of her sister's household. She glanced around the room at her surroundings. Tall mahogany bookcases laden with many first editions lined the walls. At her feet was a luxurious wool rug in the deepest red with muted swirls of gold. A crackling fire blazed in the oversized limestone fireplace, keeping the chill of the October evening at bay. Above the hearth was an artist's rendering of a classic English fox hunt, the blood-red coattails of the huntsman vividly set against a dark green backdrop of the moors, a sea of hounds at his horse's feet. Small brass lamps gave the room a soft yellow glow, and the brandy she sipped warmed her insides and made her feel sleepy.

It had been a long journey to get here and it was a relief to be off the ship and back on solid ground. She would sleep well tonight in the richly appointed room Harry's housekeeper had made up for her.

"Tell me," Lillie said, stifling a yawn and trying to focus on the reason she was back at Tynesmore. "How is it you think Lady Swindon was murdered when the police aren't investigating her death?"

"You look knackered. Are you sure we shouldn't cover this in the morning over breakfast? I don't think you will remember a thing I tell you tonight."

Lillie ignored him and continued. "Isn't it possible that your friend, what's his name, is mistaken?"

"Edgar. You see? You have forgotten his name already," Harry chided. "No, I don't think he is mistaken. The doctor attending to Lady Swindon suggested she had been poisoned. She had all the symptoms—internal bleeding, sores all over her body, hair loss. An autopsy was performed and it confirmed that she had indeed suffered a type of poisoning, but they couldn't definitively say which variety of poison was used."

"I suppose it is possible it was an accident, and she was exposed to some type of household poison she was unaware of, " Lillie mused. Her eyes felt like they had sand in them and she fought to keep them open.

"But unlikely."

"Well," Lillie continued, "not as unlikely as the theory that she had an enemy out there who was successful in killing her."

"I knew her a little when Edgar and I were younger. She was a beautiful woman. I suppose she may have had suitors, although she didn't seem the type to be unfaithful. Perhaps it was a classic 'jilted lover' situation."

"What about him, Lord Swindon?"

"I don't know him at all. It is a sensitive topic to broach though, don't you think?"

"Asking about extramarital affairs? Of course, but if we are going to get to the bottom of it, we are going to have to ask a lot of uncomfortable questions. You have to be prepared to ruffle a few feathers."

"That is why I decided to bring you in, my dear. Nobody bats an eye when an American asks rude and inappropriate questions. It is par for the course." Harry smiled and she rolled her eyes at him.

"Where exactly does the newspaper come into all this? We could just investigate quietly on our own, as a favour to your friend Ivan."

"Edgar," Harry corrected.

"Right. So why do we need to have a story published and drag up all the old heartache and anguish for the family again?"

"Between you, me, and the portrait on the wall, the story in the paper is just meant to stir the pot with the police. If we can get the Constabulary to reopen the case out of sheer humiliation it is more likely to be solved by them than by us poking around like a couple of bungling sleuths in a Doyle novel."

Lillie took some time processing this logic. She supposed Harry was being partly truthful about exposing the shortcomings of the police, but she also believed the newspaper had been a cover story to get her to come back to England. She decided not to confront him about it, since as the day had worn on, her happiness at being back in Oxfordshire had increased exponentially.

It could have been partly related to the brandy she had consumed, but for the first time in years she felt useful, something she hadn't felt in New York. There, she was a social appendage to her sister and Floyd's extravagant lifestyle. In England she was her own person and was able to be judged on her own merits—admittedly odd in a country preoccupied with class. Lillie also suspected that Harry knew she loved a mystery. It had been the perfect subterfuge to get her back.

"It could be dangerous." Lillie yawned again.

"Not to worry. We have Constance on our side. If anyone comes near you, she will growl like a rabid dog and guard your safety with her life. She is loyal to the last."

Lillie looked down at the enormous hound, who was stretched out fast asleep in front of the fire. She wasn't sure, but she thought she heard the faint murmur of a snore. "Somehow she is less ferocious than her namesake."

"The Countess Markievicz is a fervent Irish nationalist, I will give you that. And incidentally, did you not think when you named Constance before you left for New York that it would be very odd for a member of the English aristocracy to have a dog named after a Sinn Fein suffragette?"

Lillie giggled. "Not at all. It makes you look very modern and is a great opening topic at cocktail parties. How are things going with Beatrice, by the way?"

"Don't even ask. My mother is so fixated on making the perfect match that she has completely disregarded my own happiness. Why do you think I never visit London? I am afraid if I step foot off a train at Paddington Station, I will be married by tea time."

Lillie looked sleepily at Harry. It was no wonder Beatrice was enamoured with him. It was hard to believe any woman wouldn't find him attractive. His deep-blue eyes and blond hair set off his clear skin to perfection. He wasn't an overly tall man, but his height was perfectly suited to his lithe body and he dressed it with care and attention. At twenty-nine years old, his eyes were developing little crinkles around them. They gave his face an air of sophistication that was noticeably absent in the rest of his personality. That, in particular, was what made him so enjoyable to be around. He was never too serious, and found humour in almost every situation, even the most desperate. She loved him like the brother she had never had. He was steadfast for her, reliable and trustworthy, with a dash of the mischievous.

"Go to bed." Harry said, watching Lillie's eyes droop. "Tomorrow, you shall go and reunite with Jeremy Winston at the paper and we will get rolling with this charade."

With that, they both finished the last of their drinks and made their way to their respective beds.

THE FOLLOWING AFTERNOON Lillie hurriedly made her way down Cornmarket Street and into the offices of the Oxford Daily Press. She had a slight headache from drinking too much brandy and had, much to her dismay, slept for over twelve hours. Harry hadn't woken her and now she was running late for her one o'clock meeting. It was hardly the impression she wanted to make on her first day back at the newspaper.

Jeremy Winston's secretary led her into his office and asked if she could bring her a cup of tea, which Lillie politely declined. She didn't think it would do to be late *and* languishing over a cup of tea when her boss arrived.

"Lillie! Delightful to see you again. How long has it been? Two, three years?" Jeremy rushed forward to shake her hand as he kicked closed the door behind him. He removed his coat, rolled up his shirt sleeves, and took a seat across the desk from her.

Lillie smiled at him. She had grown to like Jeremy, although he had been a tough boss who had expected perfection and long hours. "Two, yes, two years. Time certainly flies by, doesn't it?" She didn't really mean it. The years since Jack's death had crawled by at a snail's pace.

"So, I won't ask what brings you here—let's dispense with the formalities and get right to it. Crime section; are you up for it?"

"I am. Harry is convinced there is a story here. The death of Lady Swindon seems to be...well, curious."

"Mm, so I hear," Jeremy looked pensive. "You haven't done this before though, have you? I mean, reported on crime."

"No, but that doesn't mean I can't do it. I realize I was only in editing the last time I was here, but I can write—quite well, actually—and I am willing to put in the time and effort to investigate." Lillie didn't want to give him an inch. She had the feeling he was trying to back out of the arrangement Harry had made with him.

"Good, good," he replied quickly. "Here is the thing...I have some reservations— not about the writing, I know you are an excellent writer. It's more about the *nature* of the work."

"Oh, how so?"

"Well," Jeremy said, looking uncomfortable. "It's rather, well, dangerous. Or it can be. Why, just last month I had one of my reporters hospitalized after he did a piece on corruption in the army. It was an expose on war profiteering, kickbacks, that sort of thing. Anyway, a gang of thugs was waiting for him outside his house when he returned home from work one night and, well...he was seriously injured. And he was a man! Imagine what damage they could inflict on a woman!" He leaned forward for emphasis.

Finding Jeremy's dramatics endearing, Lillie stifled a smile. "I see. I am not particularly fond of shying away from a fight if that that is what is needed to uncover a truth. I may not be a man, as you point out, however, I am wise enough to be very careful. And don't forget who put us both up to this: Harry. So, you can reasonably assume he will be with me every step of the investigation. Shall we get down to specifics, then?" Lillie didn't want to give Jeremy any more time on the matter. She wasn't afraid. She had been duly warned—and would certainly heed the warning—but she was ready to get down to business.

"All right, so long as you know what you may be getting yourself into."

"I do. Now, do you see this being a regular weekly column?" Lillie pulled a notebook and pencil out of her bag.

"Yes, at least for now, and I will give it a place on the front page. Give an overview of the case in the first column— specifics of what happened, timeline, suspects, role of the Constabulary..."

Lillie nodded and scribbled notes as Jeremy talked. "The subsequent columns will necessarily follow your investigation. Don't give your readers too much information and overwhelm them. Keep it logical and precise. Paint a picture, if you will, and keep your brush strokes short."

"Got it."

"You will get resistance from the Constabulary. Expect it. Interview the officers assigned to the case first, if you can. And move outwards, expanding your investigation from there— friends, family, household staff."

Lillie nodded. "They won't like a woman poking around."

"No, they won't, so use that to your advantage in any way you can. Also, go back and read a few of the past issues, so you can follow the format of the crime reporting sections."

"Thank you for giving this a home, Jeremy. I don't think you will be disappointed," Lillie said, putting her pencil and note-book back in her bag and standing up to shake Jeremy's hand.

"Just be careful," Jeremy said, frowning. He stood up to get the door for her.

"I will." Lillie manufactured a reassuring smile entirely for his benefit. She was beginning to feel nervous, but would do everything she could to hide it. This column was a chance for her to do something. Something important.

Over the past two years in New York she had done some small bit pieces for local magazines on fashion and home keeping, but this was different. This was meaningful work. A critique of the Constabulary was not only a community based piece, it was a political commentary on the role of authority in a world changed by war. The blissful naivety of imagined innocence now replaced by food stamps, disease, suffragettes, and unemployment. Life would never be the same as it was before the war.

She glanced at her watch as she made her way onto the street and realized she was now running late for lunch with Harry. They had decided to meet at a neighbourhood pub after her meeting at the newspaper, and she still had a few blocks to walk. Picking up her pace, she quickly turned a blind corner and ran smack into a child. He fell down with a thump and immediately began laughing. His mouth was full of candy.

"Oh goodness gracious, I am terribly sorry!" Lillie cried, picking up and dusting off the boy, who looked to be about ten years old. The child continued to giggle and looked thoughtfully up at her as she busily looked him over and made sure there were no injuries.

"I am fine, Miss, thank you," he assured her. "Most important thing is you didn't spill my jellies." He held up a paper bag full of candy for her to see.

"Ah, what a relief, that would have been a terrible tragedy. Tell me young man, are you out here on the sidewalk all alone?"

"No Miss, my governess is in the shop with my sister. But she takes *forever* to pick out her sweeties. For-ev-er!" He drew out the word, rolling his eyes to the sky for maximum effect. "Pores over each and every jar, she does. I tell her, 'For the love of Pete, make up your mind, Georgie'—that's short for

Georgina but she doesn't care much for the long version. I'm William, by the way. But you can call me Will if you like, most people do. Eventually. Except Papa that is, he says it isn't proper to shorten names."

"Lovely to meet you, Will." They shook hands and Will offered Lillie some of his candy. "I really shouldn't, I am on my way to lunch and I am in a bit of a hurry..." Lillie glanced at the shop behind them, which was delightfully cheerful; jars of rainbow coloured candy lined the window shelves, the front steps were painted a pale robin's egg blue, and the sign above the door read "Sweetie Pie's Sweets" in mint-green letters. She turned back to Will, "I really must get on my way as I am terribly late. Will you be fine here until your governess comes?" Before he could answer, she heard a voice behind her.

"Lillie? Lillie Mead! Is that you?" Lillie looked up to see her old friend Primrose coming out of the candy store, holding the hand of a small girl smartly dressed in a lilac dress and holding a lollipop in her hand.

"Primrose! I should have guessed you would be the governess who takes her charges to the confectionary! How are you? Oh, I have missed you so much." She hugged her and stood back to have a look at her. "You are as beautiful as ever. Even more so." Primrose still had the same pink full cheeks and shiny dark hair, which she had demurely pinned at the nape of her neck.

"I didn't know you were back in England! When did you arrive?"

"Only yesterday, and it has been a bit of whirlwind. I didn't even have time to write to you to tell you I was coming. I am staying with Harry at Tynesmore. Have you seen much of him over the past few years? I can't believe it has been that long since I have seen you last."

"No, I haven't." She looked uncomfortable and Lillie knew she was thinking of the awkwardness of the affair she had had with her employer. "The last I heard he was very nearly engaged to Beatrice Moreton."

"Well, I don't know about that. Harry engaged to anyone isn't something I can very easily imagine. Listen, I am going to meet him for lunch now and I am late. Why don't you come by Tynesmore later tonight for supper? I know Harry would love to see you. He'll even send a car for you, I'm sure of it. What time are you off duty?"

"6 o'clock. Do you think he would want to see me? I mean, of course I want to come but...oh, never mind my rambling, that would be delightful. I am still in the same flat I shared with you. Didn't have the heart to give it up."

"Wonderful, I will see to it the car arrives for you at half past six. See you tonight. Goodbye, Will and Georgie. Enjoy your sweets!"

SHE ARRIVED at the pub a few minutes later, flustered and now quite late after her run in. She spotted Harry and a dark-haired man sitting at a small table for three by the window and hurried across the room, narrowly avoiding the closely packed tables. Both men stood up as she approached.

"I thought we agreed on lunch, Lillie—it is very nearly dinner now," Harry scolded.

"Yes, I know, and I am terribly sorry for the delay—you won't believe who I ran into..." she began. Harry cut her off before she could continue.

"Let me introduce you to Edgar Swindon, Lady Swindon's son."

"Oh, hello, very pleased to meet you. I am terribly sorry for your loss, Mr. Swindon," Lillie said, gently shaking his hand.

"Thank you, and please, call me Edgar." He smiled at her and pulled out her chair so she could sit down beside him. Once she was seated, he took his chair and continued. "I owe you an enormous thank you for coming all this way to help me find out what happened to my mother. It is a frightfully long journey from New York City."

"Not at all, and I am not sure if I will be any help, I'm afraid. But I will certainly do my best to get the Constabulary to sit up and take notice. Further to that, I have just come from a very fruitful meeting with Jeremy Winston from the newspaper. He has agreed to run a weekly column on the front page where I shall report on our progress in the case."

"Well done. That is what I was hoping for," Harry said.

"Me, too. Next order of business is to interview the constable who was put in charge of the initial investigation. Edgar, forgive me for getting right down to it, but do you remember who he was?"

"There were two. One was a Constable Worley, I believe. I can't remember the name of the other chap. Father might. I'll ask him."

Lilly pulled a leather-bound notebook from her brown shoulder bag and began to write notes. "Good, that is a start. How far did they go in their investigation?"

"From what I could see, not very far at all. They spoke briefly to the coroner, who confirmed that Mother was indeed exposed to something that was poisonous, but he couldn't specify what. The officers came to the house and poked around the kitchens and an old gardening shed and concluded nothing was obviously amiss. They asked Father some questions, nothing too earth shattering, and then the last I heard Constable Worley had been suspended for something or other and we never heard from them again."

"Seems very cursory," Harry said.

"I agree," Edward replied. "Extremely disappointing."

"You don't know why Constable Worley was suspended?" Lillie asked.

"I don't, no. I called around the station a few weeks later to see where the investigation was at and the response I got was that Worley wouldn't be back for six months. When I asked who would be taking over his cases, I was told in no uncertain terms that they considered Mother's death an accident and wouldn't be proceeding with the investigation."

"It seems then the first order of business is to track down this Constable Worley and find out more about his initial investigation. Next I should like to speak with your father, Edgar. Would that be possible?" Lillie asked.

"Certainly. Would you like to come to Wrenhaven tomorrow? I will see to it that he is available. Perhaps around two o'clock?"

"Yes, that would helpful. And in the morning I shall track down our Constable Worley and see what he has to say for himself."

"Shall we order?" Harry waved over their server. "I am ravenous."

The three of them spent the next hour chatting about their school days. Because Edgar had studied engineering at Oxford, his classes had been held across campus from Lillie's, and she had never met him. Harry, by contrast, seemed to know everyone from all departments. Lillie wondered if he had done more socializing than studying at school. Harry had a wonderful knack for imitation and he entertained them by doing improvisations of some of their professors. By the end of it, Edgar and Lillie found themselves in stitches, much to the dismay of the surrounding patrons. It was good to really enjoy herself. She watched Edgar wiping the tears of laughter from his eyes and thought he must be feeling much the same. After the grief of death, laughter was therapeutic.

Once or twice, Lillie thought fleetingly of who could be a suspect in the death of a lady. She knew household staff and family must be considered as a matter of priority. Watching Edgar, she had a hard time believing he could have had anything to do with it, although she knew she mustn't dismiss someone just because they had made a good first impression. Everyone must be considered, no matter how honest they seemed.

From time to time throughout lunch, Lillie found herself thinking about Jack. She tested herself by thinking of him for only a few seconds at a time. If she kept her reminiscing short, she could just manage to escape unscathed from her memories. If she lingered too long, she knew she would feel a wave come over her, stifling her breath and hollowing out a hole inside her. The mind was a powerful thing.

Harry hadn't mentioned Jack since she had arrived. It was as though he feared if he did, she would vanish back to America again. She didn't mind. She wasn't sure she was ready to loosen the reins on her recollections and have them run rampant. Some things were better left unsaid.

They finished their lunches and Lillie and Harry said goodbye to Edgar, agreeing to meet the following afternoon at his house. Rumple was waiting patiently by the car for the return journey to Tynesmore. Once inside, Lillie rested her head back against the dark green leather seat of the Rolls Royce and closed her eyes for a few minutes, almost nodding off before she remembered her meeting with Primrose.

"Harry, I completely forgot, but I invited Primrose to join us this evening for dinner. I am sorry to take liberties, but she won't be expecting anything grand at all—just a little reminiscing. You don't think the cook will be upset, do you? What with us not telling her until now?"

"Absolutely not. How delightful, I have missed Primrose and I adore impromptu gatherings. I'll send the car 'round for her. Perhaps we should have asked Edgar to join us as well—that would be a capital match."

"Careful, Harry, you are sounding like your mother there."

"Quite right. I shan't say another word for fear of becoming presumptuous and narrow minded."

"Too late."

THAT EVENING, Primrose arrived at Tynesmore at 7:30 p.m. sharp, driven by a perfectly coiffed Rumple in the immaculate Rolls Royce which, to Lillie's surprise, had been hurriedly washed and dried that afternoon by Harry himself.

Lillie carefully watched Primrose's reception in the foyer, standing back to allow her and Harry to exchange pleasantries. She knew Harry was nervous, although he would hardly admit it to her. He had consumed two strong whiskeys and half a bottle of wine before their friend had arrived in a seeming effort to calm his nerves. It was surprising he could still string a sentence together, but he was the picture of tranquility. The only giveaway was his hands as he twisted them together or clasped them together behind his back or tried to make them lie flat against his sides in order to stop their trembling. Lillie couldn't even begin to imagine what a wreck he would have been had he not consumed so much alcohol. *Astonishing*, she thought.

They sat in the dining room for the duration of their delicious, three-course meal, chatting companionably, and then made their way to the drawing room after dinner to sip their sherries in front of the fire. While Harry fiddled with the gramophone in the corner of the room, Primrose leaned forward and clasped Lillie's hand.

"Tell me, how are are you really?" She kept her voice low and gave Lillie's hand a squeeze.

"As well as can be expected. I surprised myself by coming here. I wasn't going to, but Harry insisted...and I am glad I did." Lillie watched the flames dance in the fireplace, her vision becoming blurred by the heat and the sudden watering of her eyes.

"I am glad you did, I feared I would never see you again after...well. You loved him, and he loved you. Very much indeed. For that you must be grateful."

"I suppose I am. Although I can't help but feel—well, that I wasted time. You remember...I didn't know, not right away, and I must have hurt him..." Lillie looked away and closed her eyes.

"I remember that you were enjoying the company of a young man whom you thought you were going to marry, and that Jack was just a friend. How were you to know right away that Jack would become the love of your life? You had only just met, after all, and he took an eternity to make his move. Glaciers moved faster! You couldn't have known and when you decided to marry that young man... gosh, what was his name?"

"Andrew."

"Right, Andrew. Well, anyway, you couldn't have known then that Jack was in love with you, because he never said anything."

"Yes, but when he did finally tell me he loved me, instead of jumping into his arms, I told him I was engaged to be married and he needed to respect that. I was a fool, don't you see?"

Primrose frowned. "What I see is a woman who chose to keep her vow to a man whom she had agreed to marry. When Andrew exposed himself, albeit unwittingly, as the womanizing sod he was, you did the right thing and cut him loose."

"Well, none of it matters now anyway, does it? Jack is dead, and I wasted what time I could have had with him on an undeserving subject." Lillie shook her head in remorse.

"Wrong. You and Jack shared some wonderful times before he died. He loved you very much. Let us all be thankful for the time we had with those we loved." Primrose smiled encouragingly at her.

Lillie hoped she would one day come to the same conclusion as Primrose, but for the time being she had more regrets than she knew what to do with.

Harry finally found the music he was looking for. The deep, haunting sound of a lonely saxophone filled the air; the black, newly frosted October sky stretched endlessly beyond the leaded glass drawing room windows. Lillie sat stone still by the fireplace, lost in a swirling torrent of memories.

7

LILLIE

FTER A LATE NIGHT REMINISCING with Primrose, Lillie and Harry made their way the following morning to the address given to them by the local police station.

Constable Worley lived on the outskirts of Oxford in an area peppered with bungalow housing that had seen better days. The Rolls Royce, still gleaming from Harry's polishing, was conspicuous against its surroundings. Rumple pulled up in front of a peeling wooden fence, beyond which was an overgrown garden and a dilapidated cottage with a faded number sign reading 25 Millbury Lane.

As she and Harry got out of the car, they were immediately hit with the stench of a privy and the sound of children whining. Harry made a face and started to protest, but Lillie preempted him by putting a forefinger up to her lips. Opening a squeaky gate hanging by the barest of threads, they proceeded down a broken stone path and knocked on a knotted and ancient front door. It was opened by a middle aged woman wearing a dirty grey dress, on top of which she had fastened an apron that might have once been white, but was now a dilapidated shade of ivory.

"And what do you want?" she barked inhospitably.

"We have come to see Constable Worley. The station gave us this address," Harry said.

"Ha, a constable he ain't no more is he?" She ran her words together in a mean slur and Lillie began to think they had made a mistake coming. She glanced at Harry to see if he were deterred, but his lips were set in a firm line and he wasn't showing the least inclination of backing down.

"I should like to speak with him, and I don't have all day to stand here discussing his professional situation. Is he here or isn't he?" Harry demanded.

"Oh, all right," she said, retreating. "Aye, he is. Don't supposed you want to come in, do ya? Get those fancy clothes dirty, you will." She laughed, exposing a mouthful of decaying teeth.

"No, thank you, we don't wish to be an inconvenience. We will wait in the garden for him." With that he turned on his heel and made his back towards the gate with Lillie trailing behind him.

As they waited, Lillie wandered to the side of the house and peered around the corner and into the backyard. Tall stinging nettles hindered her mobility, but she was able to get a good view of a run-down outbuilding with its large, sagging front doors flung open. Inside, chickens pecked the dirt floor around some old tools and a few moldy looking bales of straw.

What was of particular interest to her was something half covered under a dirty canvas tarpaulin. She could just make out the shape and the front handlebars of what appeared to be a brand new Triumph motorcycle. Its steel was polished to a shine and there was not a speck of grime on the tires. She quickly made her way back to the front yard to where Harry stood talking to Rumple over the fence.

A few more minutes passed before a stout and disheveled man made his way from the cottage and lumbered over to where they were waiting.

"Good morning. What can I do for you?" Worley asked kindly. He had better manners than his wife, and although his appearance was hardly police-like, he did exude some semblance of capability.

"Constable Worley, pleased to meet you. I am Harry Green and this is Lillie Mead from the Oxford Daily Press. Ms. Mead is writing a story on the death of Lady Swindon and we wanted to get in touch with you, as I understand you were the lead investigator on the case."

"I was, yes. Although truthfully there wasn't really much of a case. Obvious signs of poisoning, to be sure, but the conclusion was it was likely from a household product."

"Really? And did you find that particular product in your search?"

Worley began to look uncomfortable with the direction of the conversation. He glanced around, avoiding eye contact. "We didn't, no."

"Well, that is strange," Harry continued. "Don't you find that strange?" He looked to Lillie as though confused.

She didn't wait for Worley to answer. "If it were my case, I certainly think I would either try to find this household product or carry on with the hypothesis that perhaps someone intentionally gave Lady Swindon poison. Incidentally, did you interview the house staff?"

"Look, the both of you, the police investigated and the result was what I just said. Case closed."

"So you did not interview the house staff?" Lillie confirmed.

Worley was becoming increasingly agitated. "Just what is it that you are planning to print, Ms. Mead?" he said aggressively, changing the subject.

"I plan to print the truth, Mr. Worley," Lillie answered,

purposefully not addressing him as Constable. "That the Constabulary appears to have dropped the ball in the case of Lady Swindon's death. That the investigation was done with a minimum of inquiry, and that the lead investigator in the case has been suspended from the force. Why is that, by the way?"

"I don't see how that is any of your business."

"Perhaps it isn't, Mr. Worley. But I plan to print this story regardless, so the more information you give me, the more favourably I can represent you. If you choose to be a hindrance instead of a help, you won't like the way you appear on paper."

"Is that a threat? Are you threatening me?"

Lillie turned the question back on him. "*Is* there someone threatening you, Mr. Worley?"

He didn't seem surprised at the question, but now looked even more uncomfortable. Not answering, he looked over instead at Rumple, who was standing at attention beside the car, eyes fixed on a spot in the distance and trying very hard to appear as though he weren't eavesdropping.

"Tell me," Lillie continued. "Is that your motorcycle in the shed behind the house?"

Worley visibly jumped, his eyes widening. "That is none of your business!"

"Perhaps not, but I wonder..." she trailed off, pausing for effect. "How does a suspended Constable afford a brand-new motorcycle? In fact, how does any Constable afford a new Triumph? Here's a theory: they don't. Not unless they are on the take. So let me ask you again, Mr. Worley, is that your motorcycle?"

Worley dropped his head into his hands, covering his face. Lillie could see his hair hadn't been washed in a while, and the back of his neck was covered in a thin layer of grime that mottled his skin. She felt sorry for him. He lived in a hovel with a menacing wife and a pack of whining children. It wasn't surprising he would lose his way and venture over to the more lucrative dark side. She didn't see him as a bad man particularly—just a lost and desperate one.

Adopting a kinder, gentler tone, she continued. "Mr. Worley, a woman is dead. Most likely she has been murdered. You can still do the right thing and help uncover the truth about her death. Obviously someone is paying you to keep quiet, and I assure you in the long run this isn't the path you want to take. The Swindons are a powerful family and they will gather all their considerable resources to ensure this case is solved."

Harry nodded in agreement. "They will, old chap. They will. There is no win here for you."

Worley was obviously wrestling with his thoughts. He rubbed his forehead as though the answer to his predicament could be massaged out. The sound of a door slamming inside the house broke him out of his trance. "I don't know the man's name, the one who offered me the money."

"Where did you meet this man?"

"At the races. During the betting, this chap comes over to me and asks for an update on the Swindon case. That in itself was strange, since there hadn't been any press on it yet, so I just told him we were investigating and it was confidential. I thought he had some nerve, asking an off-duty constable about a murder investigation. Inappropriate. Anyway, I was betting on the two o'clock race, as I do, and he waited around long enough to see that I lost it, something I could hardly afford. So I guess he saw a way in, I am ashamed to admit. He offered me two hundred pounds to get myself suspended from the force for a few months and throw the investigation."

Lillie and Harry looked at one another. Harry raised his eyebrows and asked, "How did he propose you get yourself suspended?"

"Told me if I got squiffy—you know, had too much drink—
and lost my handcuffs, the office would suspend me for being
disorderly in public. Similar thing happened to another officer
before, a couple of years back. You probably read about it, it
was in all the papers and, well—you know how these things go,
public outcry and all that. The Constabulary had no choice but
to suspend him. Anyway, I figured I had to make a scene, and so
I did, in order to get noticed. It was the perfect venue for it as I
had just lost all my quid. I made a ruckus with the bookies and
pushed a few people on my way to the bar. Then I made a show
of falling down in front of a crowd and dropped my handcuffs
and baton. Anyway, it worked. The man slipped me an envelope of cash as I was being thrown out by the security thugs
and, well...you know the rest. Now I am stuck at home with the
old wife and my kids yelping like a pack of dogs all day,"
Worley finished, hanging his head in remorse.

"So you didn't even get a first name for the man who paid
you?" Lillie asked.

"No, he didn't want to give one, though I asked. Tall guy,
thinning hair but not old. Wore a suit, nothing too fancy, not
Savile Row or anything like that. Not that I would be a good
judge. Never had a decent shirt to wear in my life, save for my
uniform."

"Did he say why he wanted you to throw the case?" Harry
asked.

"No, not really. Said it would be best if the Constabulary
focused on other things. He said that Lady Swindon's death
wasn't anything needing investigation."

"And you believed him?"

"No, not really. But he wasn't a sinister type. He seemed a
little nervous himself. Like he didn't really want to be there, like
he didn't want to be buying a constable's favours. So I guess I
wanted to believe him. To that point we hadn't really found

anything concrete in Lady Swindon's death and I didn't really think she was the type to go and get herself murdered, so I figured maybe the guy was telling the truth. And if I could profit a bit from it, why not?" He paused. "Sounds terrible now I that I hear it with my own ears, though, it really does."

"Do you know where we might find this nameless man?" Harry asked.

"I got the feeling he wasn't from around these parts. Asked for some directions to get back to the train station at one point. If I would have to guess, I would say London."

"And no idea where we could begin to track him down. Nothing at all to track him by?" Harry was getting irritated.

Worley scratched his head and thought for a moment. "Can't say I can think of anything."

"But the money was in a envelope, correct?" Lillie interjected.

"Yes, I still have it, the envelope that it is. Most of the money is gone though. It was enough to buy the Triumph and then some. I wanted the freedom of being able to just leave this place. Hence the motorcycle." He looked down at the ground and kicked at the dirt with the toe of his shoe, unable to meet their eyes.

"Can I see the envelope?" Lillie asked, thinking there might be some mark on it with which they could track the man. Worley nodded and went to fetch it, returning with an ivory-coloured envelope. He handed it over to Lillie, who noticed he had removed the remaining cash. She looked it over and could see the faintest trace of a watermark symbol.

"Do you mind if I keep this?" she asked.

"Not at all. I suppose this means you are going to splash my sins all over tomorrow's paper, then?"

"I will be discussing this case, yes, and I will report the truth —that you have been helpful in aiding our investigation and are to be commended for doing so. I don't see the need to dredge up past wounds if they aren't relevant."

A wave of relief washed over Worley's face. He even managed a small smile.

"Thank you, miss. That is kind. Please, allow me to help in whatever capacity I can behind the scenes. I would like to right my wrongs and help find out what really happened to Lady Swindon."

"Thank you Mr. Worley. One never knows when a police officer might come in handy. I shall keep your offer in mind," Lillie said, smiling.

They said their goodbyes. Harry and Lillie seated themselves back inside the car and looked at each other with incredulity as Rumple eased away from the cottage.

"Well done!" Harry enthused. "Your deductive powers are astonishing! I knew you were the man for the job."

Lillie laughed. "But just exactly *who* do you think wants a murder investigation quashed?"

"The person responsible, naturally."

"And don't you find it just the slightest bit odd that Lady Swindon's death became a closed case when Worley got himself suspended? I mean, why wouldn't the file just be transferred to the next officer?"

"I would hazard a guess that whoever killed Lady Swindon has friends in the Oxford Constabulary—that's the most likely scenario. Have you any idea on where the envelope may have come from? "

"Not yet, but I'll get working on it. Most people don't realize it, but stationery is stamped, and watermarks are like calling cards—they can often be traced."

"I wouldn't have thought of that. I never give paper a second thought," Harry said, looking pleased. "Lunch and then to the Swindons'?"

"Absolutely. I am famished."

Lillie let out a sigh and stared out the window as the car rejoined the main road into town and gathered speed. The smell of the woodsmoke that had curled through the car windows was layered now with a thin veil of apprehension; she felt increasingly uneasy about what awaited them after lunch.

8

LILLIE

WRENHAVEN HALL WAS A majestic grey manor that loomed over a sapphire-blue lake flanked both east and west by towering cypress trees. The building stretched out and back in the shape of a squared horseshoe, and although the home dated to the mid-18th century, it was marvellously preserved and looked as though it could have been built relatively recently.

Beyond the house the hills rose and fell, their undulations as pleasing as the lavender-tinged sky they set off to perfection. Lillie thought to herself about the quick research she had already done on Lord Swindon. He was known to stock his lake with trout, and host an annual fishing party that was something of a legend in Oxfordshire. To receive an invitation for this exclusive weekend was a validation of one's standing in society.

As Rumple negotiated the long, winding drive to the front entrance, Harry looked pensive. "So, Worley was bribed, but we don't know by whom."

"Correct," Lillie said, absently twirling a piece of auburn hair around her finger. "It's an important part of the case, no doubt about it."

"You are probably already thinking this, but I believe we should be very tight-lipped about any clues we discover as we go."

"Indeed, the less said the better. I plan to give an overview of our investigation in the column for the newspaper, but no specifics. It won't be the easiest thing to write, come to think of it..." Lillie furrowed her brow.

"Remember, you just need to say enough to prod the Constabulary, but not enough for anyone to realize where or on who the investigation is closing in on."

"It would certainly be helpful if we *could* actually close in on someone..."

"Rumple, tell me, have you had any occasion to get to know the staff at Wrenhaven?" Harry leaned forward as he spoke, draping his arms over the front seat. While Lillie knew he didn't believe for a second that Edgar or his father had had anything to do with the death of Lady Swindon, it wouldn't do to rule anything out at this point.

"No sir, I have not. I do understand from village scuttlebutt that Lord Swindon was not affected as so many other families were by the war."

"In what regard?"

"It's said he invested heavily in machinery plants in 1913 and expanded those investments in early 1914. There was some talk that he had been tipped off by Sir Edward Grey in the foreign office that England would be going to war. Apparently he secured the family's finances for generations to come on the money he made from that machinery during the war."

"Oh, that is ridiculous. No one knew England would be at war by the end of 1914—we may have suspected it but we didn't know it. And from what I have heard about Grey, he was hardly the sort of fellow to be the least bit concerned about an acquaintance's business futures. He had far too much else on the mind. Where on earth are you getting your information, Rumple?"

"Harry!" Lillie admonished. "You asked Rumple a question and he gave you a very helpful answer. Whether or not it is gossip, it is good information to have going forward, don't you think?" She didn't wait for him to answer before adding, "Thank you, Rumple."

A quiet descended in the car as Harry fell into a sulk. Lillie watched the passing scenery outside the car window and thought about the war. It was hard to believe it had been over now for almost a year. The aftershock of all the death and destruction was still being felt heavily in England. Food shortages, maimed soldiers, and grieving families were weighing on the country's psyche.

Harry spoke up again. "My apologies, Rumple, I don't mean to snap at you. You did as I asked and provided me with information—all this talk of war profiteering in the press recently has exhausted my good patience. Have you anything else on the family from your excursions into the vortex of village gossip?"

Lillie shot him a warning glance.

"Only that the Swindons were lavish entertainers. Tommy, a footman at the house, told Mae from the post office that Lord Swindon hired the entire London Philharmonic Orchestra to play for Lady Swindon's birthday last year. They had not fewer than 200 guests for the occasion. Apparently there was a couple in attendance from the city who tried to swim the length of the lake in their evening dress on a bet. The lady had to be rescued by her own chauffeur once she got into trouble. Such scandal. If I didn't know better, I would have thought them Americans... my apologies, Miss. I don't mean to give offence."

"Offence is taken, not given, Rumple. And thank you for your candour." Lillie smiled at the back of Rumple's head.

"Well, Lord Swindon must have loved Lady Swindon very

much indeed to throw such an extravagant celebration for her," Harry said.

"That is the consensus, yes. Mae from the post office thought them a very happy couple indeed. Apparently they loved to travel regularly to London and stay in the finest hotels. Lord Swindon spent as much time buying her gifts and dresses in Selfridges and the like as anything else. She was something of a jewelry aficionado. Had pieces from all over the world, and word is, her collection is worth quite a fortune." The three of them fell silent as Rumple pulled the car up to the front entrance.

Up close, Wrenhaven Hall was even more impressive than from at a distance. Its roof was topped with a series of minarets with turquoise zinc caps and gold pinnacles. The sheer size of the building was staggering. The house boasted near floor to ceiling windows on not only the first floor but on the second and third as well. The grey stone facade was completed with the utmost of care, each stone melded perfectly into the next, its mortar barely visible to the eye.

A tall, slim butler opened the colossal oak front doors, greeting them with a bare minimum of interest before leading them to the library. As they walked through the foyer Lillie couldn't help but glance up to the second floor landing. Above her were a series of frescoes, their colours—although faded with years of exposure to light from the windows—set off the honeyed oak floors and panelled walls to perfection. Silken rugs beneath their feet muffled the sound of their shoes as they walked the long length of the hallway to the library. The butler showed them into the large and lavish room, nodded almost imperceptibly, and closed the door behind him as he left.

Harry leaned over and whispered. "Makes Tynesmore look like a hovel!"

"Hardly. But it is rather grand, isn't it? I don't think I have ever seen a house so magnificent. I'm not sure it feels much like a home though...perhaps a home for royalty, but certainly not for the average chap. Listen—while we are alone, how do you wish to proceed with our visit today? Shall we just interview Edgar and his father, or shall we actually try to gain their permission to snoop around the house? Feels awfully invasive, don't you think?"

"Perhaps, but we haven't any choice. If we are going to try to figure out who is behind this mess, we are going to have to investigate."

"I'm not even sure what we would be looking for. And suppose they don't want us to anyway?" Lillie asked.

"Well, then, that would tell us something right there, wouldn't it?"

"I suppose."

They were interrupted by a young maid who brought in a silver tray with tea and currant biscuits. Harry assured her that they would pour for themselves and dismissed her. She quickly exited the way she had come, leaving them alone once again.

As Harry rose to pour the tea, Lillie glanced around the library. At the end of the vast room hung a large portrait framed in leafed gold. The woman in the painting stared back at her with soft, genteel eyes, her dark hair cascading over one ivory skinned shoulder. Although Lillie couldn't pinpoint the woman's age, it didn't matter—she embodied an eternal beauty, her high cheekbones and graceful neck all but timeless.

"Is that Lady Swindon?" she asked, pointing to it. Harry nodded as he stirred a few lumps of sugar into his tea and held his cup up to the light to inspect it carefully.

"Beautiful woman, wasn't she?" he said absently as he turned the cup in his hand. "Edgar bears much resemblance to her."

"Quite a necklace she is wearing. Ruby? Look at the size of

the drop, Harry. I don't think even Queen Mary has a stone that large in all the Crown jewels."

"You heard what Rumple said: a jewel aficionado." He continued the examination of his teacup and concluded, more to himself than anyone, "I do believe Tynesmore has better china though..."

Finished with his thorough vetting of the porcelain, he handed Lillie her tea. They sat on the edge of a dark-green, velvet sofa and sipped their drinks in silence, both lost in their thoughts as they waited.

A moment later Edgar and his father entered the library and Harry and Lillie rose for introductions. Lord Swindon was a handsome man, although very unlike his son in every way imaginable. Whereas Edgar was tall and dark, Lord Swindon was a stocky, stout man with greying, ashen-blond hair and intense, blue eyes.

"Thank you for coming," he said, his speech clipped and cold. It was obvious he would have preferred them not being there.

His discomfort visibly increased as they conversed about Lady Swindon's death; when Lillie asked him about the days leading up to it, he became flustered and got up to move about the room, picking up things and setting them back down here and there as he answered her questions abruptly and without explanation or expansion.

It became abundantly clear after a mere five minutes had passed that Lord Swindon was hardly going to be the source of information in their investigation that they had hoped for. In fact, Lillie had to take his testimony more as that of a hostile witness than of an informant. She had difficulty deciding if she felt sorry or annoyed by him. Obviously he was having a grievous time dealing with his wife's death, but she had been hoping for a rather more agreeable attitude towards their inquiry.

They continued with their questions, but Lord Swindon spent much of the time staring out the window towards the vast hills in the distance. He was so removed from their conversation that Edgar had to prompt him if his response was required, often two or three times. Lillie decided there was no use carrying on in this vein and asked one last, provoking question.

"Lord Swindon, were you and Lady Swindon happily married?"

Lord Swindon turned from where he was standing at the window and faced her head on. His face grew red with a creeping rage that began on his neck and quickly rose to his cheeks and across his forehead. His eyes flashed.

"What does a girl your age know of *marriage*?" he said, spitting the word out venomously, his anger completely startling everyone in the room. His voice rose. "Marriage is the most sacred of institutions—but it can be the most gut wrenching, lonely, painful place in the world. It is a stifling barren landscape hindering our dreams and aspirations and laying waste to all we hold dear. And yet," he said, pausing, clearly having trouble speaking. His voice became a whisper. "I loved her, I loved her..." He broke off and began to weep.

Edgar, surprised at the outburst, quickly crossed the room and went to his side. "Father, please come and sit down. This is all too much for you." He guided him to a chair and stood beside him as Lord Swindon sat with his head in his hands, great sobs escaping unstifled from his throat. He was inconsolable.

Lillie looked over at Harry, who motioned towards the door. She spoke quietly. "Lord Swindon, I am sorry for your loss and I apologize for upsetting you. I think we should take our leave. Please excuse us and accept our condolences."

Lillie and Harry made their way to the door of the library quickly and without looking back. They hurried wordlessly down the great hall to the front door. Edgar came jogging after them and arrived just as the butler was handing them their coats.

"Harry, Lillie, please forgive him. He doesn't know how to handle his grief and he lashes out. I should have warned you before you came that he would be difficult. He isn't himself—this isn't the way he was before. Some days are good and others are, well, like today. I thought he would be more helpful—I am terribly sorry. But please don't go yet. Would you like to have a look around? Or interview the house staff? You have come all this way and I should like you to have the opportunity to do a thorough inquiry."

"We would indeed like to interview the house staff, but it doesn't have to be now. I don't want to upset your father any further today," Lillie replied.

"Please, don't think of it. Come with me. I will show you around the house and have whomever you would like to speak to brought into the drawing room. This is what you came for, and Father will understand once he has the time to reflect on things." Edgar handed their coats back to the butler.

It took the better part of an hour and a half to tour the house. They started with the downstairs rooms and the basement kitchens, where the staff of the house was going about their household chores with polite nods and the efficiency of a military regiment. The main floor rooms were mostly formal, with the exception of a small comfortable drawing room located adjacent to the front entrance. A grand ballroom, a larger drawing room suitable for formal gatherings, a family breakfast room, and a formal dining room rounded out the first floor rooms. The second floor housed the family bedrooms in the main wing and the two additional wings were dedicated to guest accommodations.

The last room they came to was Lady Swindon's bedroom.

Edgar opened the large, carved, double oak doors and stood back to let them enter.

"Please, take your time," he said, motioning with his arm. "Take full liberty and go through everything." He didn't follow them into the room. Instead, he stood at the threshold of the space, looking forlorn.

Lillie began by carefully opening dresser drawers and moving Lady Swindon's things from side to side in her search. Finding nothing of interest to the case she opened her closet and continued looking through her clothes and shelves, checking in pockets and hat boxes for any semblance of a clue. After a half hour of fruitless searching, she moved to her dressing room and searched through drawers laden with scent and makeup, tortoiseshell hair brushes, silk scarves, and jeweled gloves. Still nothing. Returning to the main bedroom, she caught her eye on a tall slim varnished walnut cabinet wall mounted opposite the bed. After a look over at Edgar and a nod, Lillie carefully opened its doors. Inside, displayed on shelves and hooks backed by navy blue velvet, sat an astonishing collection of jewelry.

Edgar spoke from the doorway. "Mother was bit of a hoarder when it came to jewelry. She loved the history behind a piece, who made it, what part of the earth the gems came from, who faceted them, et cetera. She was more knowledgeable than anyone on the clarity of diamonds and coloured stones, and therefore what price point they should fetch on the open market. She has oodles of books on 'nature's perfect treasures,' as she loved to call them." Edgar smiled at the memory.

"Here is the piece that she is wearing in the portrait downstairs," Lillie said, carefully lifting a necklace out of the cabinet.

"Yes, Father bought that for her on her last birthday and the portrait was done shortly after. Quite a piece."

"I don't think I have ever seen a ruby quite this large." Lillie stared at the gem.

"It isn't a ruby actually, it is a red beryl. Quite a different family of gemstone altogether, I am told. From America, if memory serves correctly. Much like you." He smiled at her.

Lillie turned the drop, watching as the light reflected off its many facets. It was tear shaped and at least three inches long, set in gold with a pave of white diamonds circling it. The stone itself was blood red and almost perfect in its clarity. Very few inclusions and its brilliant cut made the surprisingly large stone glitter as though it were a much smaller, more vibrant one. Large stones often had the unfortunate predicament of being cumbersome and flat looking, but this one was quite the opposite.

"It is beautiful," she said, carefully putting it back in its case.

"Yes." Edgar agreed. "She wore it often. Father would tease her and say she would lose it if she didn't lock it up, but she wouldn't hear of it. It was her favourite piece."

Harry had taken charge of Lady Swindon's desk and was rapidly sorting through piles of paper. Lillie could tell from his hasty movements that he was uncomfortable snooping through the desk of a friend's mother. As he piled papers back into their corresponding drawers, he glanced over at her and shook his head. Apparently he was coming up empty handed, as was she.

By all accounts it appeared Lady Swindon had led a normal aristocratic life. Her comfortable surroundings were neat and orderly with nothing out of place. Her expensive clothes still hung in her cupboards as though she could be expected to breeze through the door at any minute and don one of her evening dresses. Outside her large windows a vast countryside revealed itself. Lillie felt suddenly sad. Edgar's beautiful mother would never set eyes on this view again.

She looked up at Edgar, still standing quietly by the door. Lillie realized that being in the room where his mother had died must be very difficult for him. She didn't want to linger any longer and draw out what was appearing to be a futile search.

"Thank you, Edgar, I think we are finished here. Perhaps I could have a quick discussion with your mother's maid and Harry could do the same with your butler, Mr...?"

"Groves. Yes, of course—although I can't produce mother's maid. She left shortly after her death. Obviously there wasn't anything for her to do as a lady's maid with two men in the house and no lady, so she moved on. But I will send for Mr. Groves right away. Why don't we have some more tea in the drawing room in the meantime?"

"Thank you. Do you by any chance know where your mother's maid went after leaving Wrenhaven?" Lillie asked.

"I can have our house manager sent for. I am sure she wrote her a reference so she would certainly know where she went."

AN HOUR later Harry and Lillie said their goodbyes to Edgar to begin their short journey back to Tynesmore.

"So nothing of use from the butler then," Harry stated, looking pensive.

"It doesn't appear so, no, but he is hardly the forthcoming sort of chap. He seems to have been carved from a granite slab instead of flesh and blood like the rest of us," Lillie mused.

"I daresay I agree. I couldn't have a man like that at Tynesmore for one minute. Deep brooding sort, rather like a character in a Dickens novel. Terribly depressing. How does Edgar stand it?"

"I don't think he has a choice—Groves is his father's man. While we are on the topic of Lord Swindon, did you not think his responses to our questions were, oh, how shall I put it...?"

"Disturbing?" Harry finished for her.

"Yes, exactly right. For having been a supposedly happily

married couple, he seems absolutely tormented. I don't mean by her death, which of course he is, but rather by her life. Is that possible? It certainly isn't the picture of happiness we heard from Rumple. Do you think something happened relatively recently in their marriage, something to warrant his anguish and anger?" Lillie asked.

"Very likely, although if so, I don't think Edgar has any idea of it. From everything he has said to me, he believes his parents had an idyllic marriage."

"We will need to get to the bottom of it, and the best place to start is with the lady's maid. One rarely can keep one's secrets from one's maids."

"To London then?" Harry asked.

"According to the housekeeper, Knightsbridge, to be exact. When do we leave?"

"Dear me, you are demanding, aren't you? All this sleuthing has made me thirsty. Shall we stop at the pub for a pint before we go home? We can discuss future travel plans over drinks and chips."

"Lead on, fearless soldier," Lillie mocked.

THE HUNTSMAN'S Horn was a small but pleasant Tudor building on the edge of the green in Winchester-on-Thames, a village due south of Oxford. Tynesmore was only a few miles outside the village, and Harry clearly frequented the town on a daily basis. Lillie noticed that the bartender waved to them as they entered and called out a booming hello, which was surprisingly echoed by a number of other men who were sitting around the gleamingly polished bar.

"Quite a regular then, are you?" Lillie teased.

"Easier to pop in here than do the extra half hour to Oxford, although apparently I should reconsider based on the welcome. Altogether too much merriment going on for my liking. Let's sit by the window. There is a view of the river from there and I want to avoid that bearded man at the bar. I seem to remember I may or may not owe him from our last snooker match and I would like to avoid finding out."

Lillie glanced at the bar to see a large burly man downing his drink in an extraordinarily ungentlemanly manner.

"Really, Harry, an earl's son not paying his gambling debts? Shameful."

"I assure you that when push comes to shove, I always make good, but that chap is a known cheater and I don't think he deserves my hard-earned money."

"Hard earned?" Lillie asked incredulously. "You must be joking. You are aware that you live at the family seat in Oxfordshire and are funded handsomely from the family coffers?"

"Hush. What will you have to drink now? Let's wave down the barmaid," Harry said, cheekily changing the subject.

The room was full of local townspeople, but it didn't take long for a pretty young waitress to make her way over their table. Fluttering her eyelashes at Harry, she spoke directly to him and ignored Lillie.

"What'll it be tonight, my lord?"

"Just a couple of pints, Maisie, thanks. Oh, and a plate of chips if you could. We are a little peckish."

She smiled seductively and turned to take her leave, giving them both a view of a backside barely covered by a minuscule skirt.

"I see the attraction at the Huntsman's Horn," Lillie laughed.

"Don't be ridiculous," Harry said, dismissing her. "Not my style. I say"—he looked distractedly over her shoulder to the far side of the pub—"is that...? Why, I think that is Primrose at that table in the far corner. Have a look."

Lillie glanced in the direction Harry was looking and saw, to her surprise, a despondent woman wiping her eyes with a handkerchief and taking large gulps of spirits.

"Oh dear, yes, it does appear to be Primrose. What is she doing here by herself? She looks terribly forlorn. I'll go get her." Lillie made her way across the room and sat down across from Primrose.

"Primrose, darling, what is the matter?"

"Oh, Lillie!" Primrose exclaimed, startled. Her face was red and puffy and what little makeup she wore streaked her face. She quickly wiped at her cheeks and reached across the table to grab Lillie's hands. "I am so glad to see you."

"What has happened?"

"Oh, Lillie, I have been sacked. That rotten Mr. Penderhurst said I wasn't fit to be Will and Georgie's governess! Not fit? *Not fit?* I said to him, you're the one who isn't fit! Never letting them have a speck of fun. He keeps them under his thumb at all times—they may as well be in the county lock up! They aren't allowed to run or play or eat sweets or do anything much fun at all. Poor poor Will and Georgie, and now I can't even see them anymore." She burst into tears again, sobbing uncontrollably. "And I'll miss them so," she wailed.

Lillie held her hand patiently, letting her get it all out. When the tears had subsided, Lillie said, "Nonsense. Once some time has passed, Mr. Penderhurst will realize the error of his ways and will be begging to have you back. You are a wonderful governess, take heart in that. In the meantime, you must pull yourself together, come over and sit with Harry and me, and forget about this mess tonight."

Primrose nodded, wiped her face, and smoothed her hair. They made their way back to the table hand in hand, where Harry rose to pull out their chairs.

"Well now," he said gently, "how about that. Fancy seeing you here, my dear. I get the pleasure of your company twice in twenty four hours." He gallantly ignored the redness on Primrose's tear-streaked face.

She sniffled loudly. "Hello, Harry."

"Primrose has had a terrible day," Lillie told him. "Apparently her employer doesn't appreciate her value and has let her go."

"What a chump," Harry commiserated. "Forget him. You will find a better job, of that I have no doubt."

"Thank you Harry, and I hope so. I'll just miss the little ones."

"Of course you will, of course you will." Harry gazed at Primrose, who was trying to pull herself together. He gently took her hand from under the table and gave it a reassuring squeeze.

"Lillie and I are going to London in a few days' time. Why don't you join us?" Harry asked her.

"Splendid idea. Please do, Primrose. It will be just like old times..." Lillie stopped short, realizing with a sudden ache that one member of their past foursome was forever missing.

Harry was quick to jump in, obviously realizing the direction of Lillie's thoughts. "It is a work-related trip, you see, related to the crime column Lillie is writing for the newspaper. Your assistance would be greatly appreciated, Primrose. And it wouldn't be all dull, we can still enjoy all the pleasures the city has to offer. It would take your mind off of the children and when you return you will be fresh and rested and have all this behind you."

"I would like that, actually. A change is as good as a rest they say," Primrose answered, looking slightly less miserable.

"Delightful! Shall we catch an afternoon train tomorrow?" Harry said, looking to Lillie, who nodded her agreement.

Lillie, thinking, turned to gaze out at the night sky through the hazy pub window. To date, their inquiries into Lady Swindon's death had produced little more than an oddly angry and grief-stricken husband, a doting but oblivious son, a corrupt police detective who had been paid off by an unknown man, a stone-faced and most unhelpful butler, and a lady's maid they had yet to find. They were hardly close to solving anything, but their lack of knowledge left Lillie with the uncomfortable feeling that they didn't have enough of the facts to know where or how they would encounter their killer.

9

THE MAN IGNORED THE WHISTLE of the kettle in the small and cramped kitchen in the red brick building on Melbury Road in London. Assuming someone else would attend to it, he continued down the hallway to his office. He removed his overcoat and hat and placed them over the back of an extra chair to dry. He never remembered to bring an umbrella, and it was no wonder he was soaked through. A cup of tea and a biscuit certainly wouldn't be turned away. He noticed his new secretary was not at her desk so, annoyed, he went to get it himself.

He made his way back down the hallway, hair dripping on his collar and soaking the back of his neck, wet shoes squeaking on the marble floors, and found the kettle still whistling. He rummaged around in the cupboard and managed to locate a chipped tea pot and some loose-leaf tea, which he set about spooning into the pot. He stared out the minuscule kitchen window while he waited for it to steep. The rain was now coming down sideways in huge waves; the wind gusted in violent spurts, swirling it this way and that. He watched as the few people remaining on the sidewalk ran for cover, collars pulled up high, purses and briefcases held over their heads for shelter.

He checked his watch. Six-thirty p.m. That would explain the empty building. With his tea poured and a few biscuits found, he headed back to his office. He wondered who had been the ninny who had forgotten to turn off the heat before leaving the office.

He kicked off his shoes and removed his wet socks. He found a pair of leather and wool slippers in his bottom desk drawer and slipped them on, thankful that he had remembered to put them there. He often kept extra clothes in his office for occasions when his work kept him from returning to his small flat in Mayfair. He removed his tie, also wet, and unbuttoned his shirt, dry but for the collar and cuffs. He pulled a dark grey cashmere sweater over his cotton undershirt. That was better. Sinking deep into his leather chair, he pulled a folded newspaper from his desk drawer.

People from his past life, those who knew him before the war, would be surprised to find him sitting in an office that looked more like a large house than it did an office building. As he drank his tea, he thought, as he did everyday, about the deception of his life. Originally, the subterfuge had been necessary—even he had seen that. And as torturous as it had been in the early days and weeks, time had healed the sharp pain of loss and turned into more of a chronic ache. The work had engrossed him, and it was meaningful. It paled in comparison to anything he had done before.

And yet here he sat, keeping up the pretence of a life that wasn't his.

He unfolded the newspaper and began to read. The London and various international papers were delivered religiously to his office on a daily basis, but the paper he was holding now wasn't as easy or timely to come by. Often he had to wait a week or more to receive it by messenger from Oxford. When it arrived he would lock it away in his desk drawer until he could be alone and without distraction. Then he would pull it out and read it from cover to cover, savouring the provincialness of village life and the simple pleasures it provided.

Watching the rain hammer the windows, he stared out to the darkened October sky and remembered a night just over two years ago. The memory was always the same, but he replayed it in his usual careful manner. It was a trait he never seemed to be able to shake, no matter how reckless or cavalier he wished he could be. Perhaps he replayed the memory in his mind because he wanted to assuage his conscience. Or perhaps he did it to ensure he hadn't missed anything.

Once again he saw the evening unfold in his memory as though it were yesterday. The venue was the ballroom of a large Mayfair home. Officers in uniform circled the room, their sweethearts hanging onto their arms afraid to let go for fear the men would vanish back to the front. Older women and their husbands greeted the dignitaries and colonels with gratitude and reverence.

As he stood on the threshold of the room, he'd wondered, not for the first time, if a surprise visit was ever a good idea. He felt inside his trouser pocket for the small silken pouch he had carefully placed there earlier that day. He knew she would be here. She had said so in her letters.

He had hoped he might be able to whisk her away from the crowded house and walk through the moonlit park across the street. It wasn't how he would have preferred to ask her, but he didn't have much time before he would be expected back in Belgium—and he wanted to secure their future together.

His eyes scanned the room in search of her. It was difficult to pick anyone out of the blossoming crowd. The laughter of the young women and their soldiers felt surreal after all he had witnessed on the battlefield. It was 1917 and the war had ground on for three excruciating years.

It was then he spotted her. She was standing with a group in one corner of the ballroom, sipping a drink and smiling as she watched couples spin around the dance floor. He was mesmerized. She wore a fawn-coloured floor length gown he had never seen before, her dark hair accented with tiny crystal pins that glinted in the candlelight. Everything about her was beautiful and understated. The sight of her reminded and assured him again of why he had come.

He began to make his way across the room towards her and wondered fleetingly how surprised she would be. They had written often over the past few years, and although he thought he knew her heart and mind, one could never be one hundred percent sure of anything.

War had certainly taught him that.

Suddenly, seeing another face he recognized across the room, he involuntarily drew a sharp breath. He blinked, twice, trying to reconcile *that face* and his current location. His mind quickly calculated. Then recalculated. There was no way the person should have been there. His thoughts raced—was he exposed, blown? Why was the person there? Had he already been seen?

Avoiding eye contact, he deftly stepped behind a large group of new arrivals and miserably watched as an American soldier walked up to the woman he loved and gave her kiss on the cheek. Startled, she looked up at the tall, fair man and smiled dazzlingly at him. She was obviously surprised and pleased to see him. The soldier grabbed her hand and pulled her onto the dance floor. For the next several minutes they swirled around the room to the music, laughing comfortably with one another. They looked as though they had known each other for some time.

As the man stood watching them, he couldn't help but have the sinking realization that he had been thrown over for this tall, blond American chap—he was her past and looked also to be her future.

Perhaps it was just as well. The face he had spotted in the crowd was a treacherous adversary and therefore the man's connection to anyone in England would certainly put them directly into harms way. He couldn't do that to the woman he loved. Maybe she would be better off with the American soldier...as utterly gut-wrenching as it was.

Stunned and unable to watch any longer, he hurried from the room. Tears welled up his eyes as he hastily tripped and bumped his way through the crowd, anxiously making his way back out onto the street. The cool night air hit his face and he began to run. He wanted to get as far away from the sounds of laughter and music as he could.

As he ran, he reached into his pocket and removed a ring from the silken pouch. Stopping, breathless, he looked down at the small but perfect diamond he had painstakingly chosen to be a symbol of their everlasting love. With all his might, he hurled it into the darkness.

After a long and sleepless night, he had left for the coast of Belgium the next morning, three days earlier than planned. Not a soul in London knew he had ever been there.

BRINGING his thoughts back to the present, the man watched rivulets of rain make their way down the window. It was getting dark and he really should be making his way home. His reminiscing had made him sad, as it often did. That night had changed the course of his life forever.

10

HARRY

WHENEVER THEY WERE IN London, Harry's parents resided in a large white-washed townhouse on the edge of St. James Park. Harry stood on the sidewalk and looked up the stairs to the glossy black front door and summoned the courage to face his mother. He had only been in London for a few days, but that was long enough without a visit that his mother would certainly be dissatisfied if she had already heard he was in town. He hoped she hadn't.

The door was answered by his parents' butler, a rigid and uptight man of at least seventy who in manner and appearance was in stark contrast to the more unorthodox Rumple. Harry was already beginning to miss him.

"Harry my darling!" His mother swooped into the room in her typically overly dramatic fashion and laid a kiss on his cheek as he stood to greet her. "How long have you been in London?" She looked around her. "And where are your bags?"

"I won't be staying here, mother, I have friends with me and I have secured us a suite of rooms at Claridge's," he said, side-stepping the question of his arrival.

"Nonsense. You must all stay here. There is plenty of room. Who is with you? Chaps from Oxford? Old school chums?"

"An American friend and another, uh, person. But never mind, how are you and father?"

"Very well, thank you. Although you know your father. Spends all his time working and not nearly enough time in idle pursuits. Why don't you come for supper this evening and see him? I'll ring around and see if Beatrice can join us. And bring the chaps who are staying with you. It will be a sort of reunion."

"Mother, I really haven't the time."

"Don't be ridiculous, haven't the time to visit with your family and your fiancée? Absurd."

"Mother, Beatrice and I are not engaged. I don't know why this is such a difficult concept for you to grasp. I am not in love with Beatrice."

"What does that have to do with anything?" she asked stubbornly.

"Quite a lot, actually. I do plan to marry for *love*. As we've discussed, I would think that you would want that for me." Harry was getting exasperated. No wonder his elder brother had escaped to Switzerland and hadn't set foot on English soil since.

"What I want, my dear boy, is for you to hurry up and be married. The longer you wait, the more difficult it is to answer questions from one's peers."

"Mine or yours?" He was needling her. "And anyway, is that really all you are concerned about? Don't you want me to be happy? Isn't a lifetime with a person you don't love signing up for torture?"

"Don't be impertinent, Harry. A marriage to Beatrice will be very favourable to you. You *can* grow to love a person, you know."

"Not bloody likely in Beatrice's case," Harry mumbled under his breath.

Ignoring him, his mother stated, "Good, it's settled then. We dine at eight. Bring your friends. Your father will be delighted to see you. Now, come and have some tea, I have so much to tell you about your brother. I've just received a letter from him. About time really—he is *hardly* the wordsmith...."

BACK AT THE hotel a few hours later, Harry ordered a whiskey from the bar and settled into a comfortable lobby armchair as he prepared to wait for Lillie and Primrose to return from their fact-finding mission. He was dreading dinner and could only imagine his parent's surprised faces when he arrived with Lillie and Primrose in tow—to say nothing of how he would fare face to face with Beatrice at long last. It wasn't that she was horrible, but Harry found her to be terribly self-important and strung as tightly as an over-tuned violin. The last time he had seen her had been at a dinner party in Oxford six months ago. He had feigned a stomachache part way through the evening and, with a ridiculous amount of relief, escaped to the pub in time to win an impromptu card game.

She had written to him a number of times since, but he had sidestepped any plans to meet her, making this excuse or that, in the hopes that she would eventually find some other prey. Aware he was behaving like a coward, Harry knew he would have to tell her that he really had no intention of getting married anytime soon—at least not to her.

He watched the hotel doorman opening the door for arriving guests, each time allowing blasts of cold autumn air into the lobby. Harry shivered and got up to move closer to the fireplace, signalling the bar for another whiskey. It was past five o'clock when he finally spotted Lillie and Primrose making their way across the lobby towards him. Their cheeks were flushed from the outdoor weather and the excited looks on their faces told him instantly they had had some success tracing the source of the elusive stationery. Harry jumped up and motioned for them to join him by the fire. As they sat down and removed their coats, Harry made his way to the bar, returning minutes later with a couple of sherries to warm them.

"You won't believe the luck we have had," Lillie exclaimed. She rubbed her hands together as much with glee as with cold and leaned in closer so they wouldn't be overheard. "Primrose and I went to three stationery manufacturers. It is truly fascinating, the whole process of how a watermark is applied to the paper. Did you know that the type of watermark can vary greatly according to which machinery is employed and how—"

Harry interrupted impatiently. "Please my dear, skip the specifics. Did you find out who manufactured this particular watermark?"

"We believe so." Primrose said, looking over to Lillie, who nodded enthusiastically.

"We most certainly did. But not only did we find out the manufacturer, we discovered, after some lengthy digging, the exact dye lot and what we believe to be the paper match for Constable Worley's envelope. It appears that the stationery in question was manufactured for and delivered to a gentleman's club on Pall Mall, the Athenaeum."

"The Athenaeum?" Harry was surprised.

"Do you know it?" Lillie questioned.

"Yes, of course. My father is a member there. Actually, I suppose I am too, now that I come to think of it. Not that I have ever used it."

"What a stroke of luck!" Primrose exclaimed. "We have been racking our brains trying to figure out how we were to gain access and have a snoop around, and now we have the perfect accomplice. You!" She smiled conspiratorially at Harry.

"So let's just have a quick review here, ladies. We believe that the man who gave the envelope of money to Constable

Worley as a bribe to behave poorly was in fact a member of the Athenaeum club. And we know this because the envelope's watermark has been traced to this particular establishment. Which means that we are are on the right track—the man was obviously from London as Worley suspected."

"Exactly. It is a good confirmation of that, to be sure," Lillie smiled triumphantly.

"Yes, but, a caution, I don't think searching the Athenaeum clubs records will be a good use of our time. They have thousands of members, and those members can, in turn, have hundreds of guests. To say nothing of the staff and delivery people. It would be impossible to trace who took a piece of stationery at some indeterminate time."

"Oh," Lillie looked disappointed, but not defeated. "I suppose it would be difficult, now you put it that way." She was quiet for a moment while she seemed to consider this. "Well then," she said determinedly, pushing on. "We are just going to have to figure out another method of tracking this man."

"I would think so, yes, and we can talk about how to do that later this evening, after we have dinner with my parents."

"Dinner?" Primrose asked hesitantly.

Harry had worried she and Lillie would be reluctant dinner goers, but he couldn't very well show up without them. It wasn't just for his mother's sake, it was selfishly for his own sake as well. He needed a buffer against Beatrice, and the two young women would certainly be that.

"Ah, yes," Harry said, clearing his throat. "My mother has invited us to dine at eight o'clock this evening and I think we should go. She was an acquaintance of Lady Swindon, you know, and she may be able to provide some additional insight into, her, ah"—here he cleared his throat again nervously —"her life." He was grasping.

He watched as Lillie and Primrose looked at one another,

Lillie raising an eyebrow. If they decided not to come to dinner, he would be in trouble. Both remained silent.

"It won't be a late evening I promise." He was hoping to stave off the mutiny he felt brewing. "Consider it a working dinner. With any luck we will get a fuller picture of Lady Swindon's life."

"Oh, all right," Lillie conceded. "But what will your mother think of you bringing the two of us to dinner? Likely she will think you are courting one of us."

Harry deftly ignored the question. "She has invited Beatrice, who shall be flinging herself at me all night no doubt," he said, trying to make light of it.

He glanced at Primrose, who had lowered her eyes and was avoiding his gaze. *Damnation*, he thought. He had obviously gone and said the wrong thing. The three of them continued to sip their drinks by the fire, hoping to find some courage within their glasses.

ARRIVING twenty minutes late that same evening, Harry, Lillie, and Primrose were shown into the drawing room of the white-washed townhouse by Lady Green's butler.

"Hello mother, father...how lovely to see you all," Harry said with forced merriment. "May I introduce my friends, Lillie Mead and Primrose Hyssop."

Three stunned faces greeted them, Beatrice's turning quickly to furious.

Harry's father recovered quickly and stepped forward. "Delighted to meet you both. When I heard Harry was bringing friends to dinner I had assumed they were school chums, but I see I was mistaken."

"Father, Lillie *is* a school chum actually—we were at Oxford together. That is where we met."

"At the university?" Harry's mother was incredulous.

"Yes ma'am, Harry and I were in a number of classes together," Lillie said, giving a her a wide smile.

"Oh!" Harry's mother exclaimed. "You are an American! Such a giveaway, your accent. Incidentally, it is customary in England to address me as my lady."

Harry quickly interjected, "Oh mother, don't be such a snob. Things are different now, and I assure you Lillie has been in England for long enough to know how things are properly done."

An awkward silence descended.

"Hello, Harry." Beatrice stepped forward, recovering, with her chin raised and her beady blue eyes set on Lillie and Primrose.

"Beatrice, hello," Harry said, quick to move on. "I say, I am ravenous, shall we go through to the dining room? Terribly sorry we are so late, seems we have missed the pre-supper drinks..." Without waiting for a reply, Harry took Primrose's arm and made his way into the adjoining room. The rest of the party followed them and took assigned seats around the table.

"Tell me, Lillie," Harry's mother began once the salad was served. "Where in the United States does your family hail from?"

"The New York area, primarily, but my parents are deceased now. My father was in the railroad business and we spent almost as much time in England as we did in America growing up." Lillie poked at her salad, pushing it around her plate.

Glancing over at Beatrice, Harry could see she had set her face into a stone-like mask, her lips in a hard line, her eyes roving over the table trying to decide which female to intimidate, Lillie or Primrose, both of whom were beginning to look as though they were birds trapped in a cage. He decided now was as good a time as any to change the conversation.

"Mother, I assume you have heard of Lady Swindon's

death?" Harry asked, wiping the corner of his mouth with his napkin and trying to look nonchalant.

"Yes, your father and I were shocked to hear of it. The Swindons have been in Oxfordshire for generations. Spanish flu, was it? Such a terrible tragedy."

"I don't think they have ruled out other causes. They haven't as yet confirmed a cause of death. You knew Lady Swindon on a social basis, did you not?"

"Yes, I did. You know, the odd luncheon here and there, or a hospital fundraiser. That sort of thing. She was a charming woman, always impeccably dressed—and those jewels! Quite a fortune she wore on a daily basis. I never liked to believe all that gossiping about her past. That sort of talk is so...gauche."

Lillie and Primrose perked up. Harry pressed the topic.

"What sort of gossip, Mother?"

"Oh, never mind, it isn't dinner conversation. Tell me, how are you enjoying the pheasant? It is so difficult to get the same quality of game in London that we are able to get in the country. Primrose, I haven't asked you, where is your family from?"

Primrose opened her mouth to reply, but Harry cut her off. He didn't want his mother to stray from the Swindon topic, and he *certainly* didn't want Primrose to be his mother's next target.

"We are all adults here, Mother—what was the gossip about Lady Swindon?"

"Oh, if you insist, Harry, although it really isn't appropriate to repeat such things."

Harry raised an eyebrow at Lillie and Primrose. Discretion was hardly his mother's forte.

His mother put her fork down and gently wiped the corners of her mouth with a napkin. "Apparently Lady Swindon had a dalliance with an Irish lad from her uncle's estate when she was young. Quite a dashing sort, I understand. Tall, dark and terribly in love with her."

"That is hardly gossip, though, is it? Certainly young love

before marriage has existed for generations." Harry purposely did not look towards Primrose.

"Well, that is the thing, my dear boy, it seems that this young love wasn't *prior* to her marriage to Lord Swindon. Quite the opposite, in fact. The dalliance occurred shortly after they were wed. And to make matters worse, this particular Irishman was seen in her company numerous times over the course of a year or so until he inexplicably vanished, never to be seen or heard from again."

"How long ago was this exactly?" Harry asked, intrigued.

"Well it must have been at least thirty years ago. Far too long ago to be of any consequence now."

Harry, Primrose and Lillie stared at one another over the table, rendered speechless by the gossip. All three were incredulous.

Oblivious to the magnitude of what had just been revealed, Beatrice spoke. "Harry, perhaps you would like to accompany me to an art exhibit tomorrow at the National Gallery?"

Before Harry could reply, his father spoke up. "Is it that Impressionism dribble on display, Beatrice?"

"I believe so, yes."

"I'm not sure it is worth a second glance, my dear. Redesdale was bang on calling the authors of those unfortunate French paintings 'art-rebels'. I should think if you do go to the exhibit you will have the place entirely to yourselves. No self respecting Englishman would dare be seen admiring anything of the sort."

Beatrice's sour mood was not improved by this exchange. Harry's father glanced his way and gave him a quick wink as the dinner plates were cleared and dessert was served.

~

By the time the trio returned to the hotel, delivered by his parents' half-asleep chauffeur, it was well after midnight.

"Hardly an early evening, Harry," Lillie admonished after they had entered the lobby and were out of earshot of the driver.

"My apologies, I thought I should never escape Beatrice's talons. Miserable girl, nose like an eagle's beak. I ask you, what on earth is my mother thinking? Does she really expect her youngest son to be happy holed up in a nest with a bird of prey constantly pecking him to death? Never mind...but what a find we made! That information on Lady Swindon certainly muddies the waters, doesn't it?"

"Tell me, how old is Edgar Swindon?" Primrose asked, stifling a yawn.

"Thirty-ish, I should think. He was a year or two ahead of me in school. Something like that." Harry nodded at the front desk clerk as they made their way to the lift. The clerk waved them over, holding up an envelope.

"A letter from Oxford, Mr. Green. It arrived with the evening post."

"Ah, thank you. Some crisis with Rumple's wardrobe, no doubt. Silly man is always wanting me to pick up this or that for him when I am in the city. Last time I was here, he requested a pair of breeches the colour of heather. Ridiculous! He hardly has the time nor the inclination to go shooting—to say nothing of how he would be teased showing up in purple trousers."

They continued on their way to the lift as Harry opened the letter.

"It is for you, my dear, from New York. Your sister sent this to the house and Rumple has forwarded it." Harry passed the envelope to Lillie, who read it silently.

"It seems Penny and her husband Floyd are planning a trip to England. They expect to arrive in London next week," Lillie reported happily.

"Oh, how nice for you!" Primrose exclaimed. "And I shall finally get to meet your family. What is the purpose of their visit? They miss you, I should expect. How long have you been gone?"

"Almost three weeks—my, how time flies. It seems Floyd has some business to attend to here and Penny wanted to join him so she could visit me."

"Where are they staying?" Harry asked. "They must plan a side trip to Oxfordshire and join us at Tynesmore."

"It doesn't say. She said she will send word when they arrive. And who knows, we may very well still be here in London next week—we have quite a lot to accomplish. Speaking of which, we really must focus on Lady Swindon's maid."

"Yes, I sent word to her mistress asking for a meeting and we have been granted her agreement—I forgot to mention it, what with that dreadful dinner on my mind this evening. We meet Agnes this Thursday at four o'clock. Apparently the lady of the house can't spare her for more than a few minutes, so we had better be prompt and to the point. Honestly, one would think slavery was alive and well in England."

"That is rich, coming from you," Lillie teased. "What sort of hours does Rumple keep?"

Harry averted his eyes downwards, hoping to avoid the question, while the lift arrived at the top floor.

"At least we were able to track her down and schedule a meeting with her." Primrose added. "Good night, Harry."

Lillie and Primrose made their way to their rooms as Harry watched them go. Primrose turned to look back when she reached the end of the long hallway, giving him a small, lingering smile.

Harry beamed. That small token of recognition was all he needed to give him a blissful night's sleep.

11

LILLIE

ON THURSDAY AFTERNOON, AT 4 o'clock sharp, Harry and Lillie rang the doorbell of a large brick townhouse in Knightsbridge. While they waited, Lillie looked out over a quiet street lined with ancient linden trees, their bare branches curving like the hands of an old woman, their canopies a reminder of the passing of time. Her sweeping vision settled on a man a few hundred feet away. He was wearing a dark-green tweed coat and lingering near a news-agent stand on the corner. For a moment, Lillie had the briefest sensation of deja-vu. Had she seen him somewhere before? Was it that morning? Or the day before? His coat had an unmistakable and memorable strand of yellow woven throughout the green. It could have been a coincidence, or perhaps she was mistaken, but she made a mental note of it anyway.

Agnes answered the door herself and showed them into a small, sparsely furnished room off the foyer that appeared to be reserved for such utilitarian tasks as receiving packages and housing coats. Lillie deduced the mistress of the house wasn't of the liberal variety and would find the thought of a maid entertaining company in her drawing room or library inconceivable.

Agnes pulled three dark, mismatched, wooden chairs out from behind an alabaster painted table and arranged them in a semi circle. Lillie got straight down to business.

"Thank you for taking the time to see us, Agnes. We realize you must be very busy, and we won't take up too much of your time."

Agnes didn't respond. She sat stone still, apparently waiting for her to continue.

"I understand you worked for the Swindons for a number of years?"

Agnes nodded, still silent.

"And that you were in Lady Swindon's employment when she passed away?"

Another nod.

"That must have been a very difficult time."

Silence.

She really wasn't getting anywhere with the young lady.

Harry raised his eyebrows at Lillie and jumped in. "Agnes, Lillie has been tasked with writing a column on the investigation for the Oxford Daily Press."

"I did hear that, yes. I still write to some of the Wrenhaven staff—we remain friends and they keep me informed." The young maid seemed surprised at her sudden willingness to talk and abruptly stopped, clasping her hands in her lap and waiting for Harry to continue.

"Yes, good, well, as it stands now, the police inquiry has been stalled, for various reasons. Well, to be more precise, it has been terminated. There exists, unfortunately, some general incompetence within the Constabulary, you see, and as a result the investigation of Lady Swindon's death hasn't been done justice. I don't want to go into the specifics here but there has been a gross miscarriage of the law. And as such, Miss Mead and I, along with the newspaper, have taken it upon ourselves to investigate what we believe to be foul play. Which is what has brought us here today to you. So, I wonder, is there anything you might have to offer? Was there anything in Lady Swindon's life that might have made her a target for murder?"

The word *murder* seemed to shock Agnes. Lillie recognized a glimmer of fear on her face. They waited in silence for a few moments. Agnes fiddled with the tie on her apron, winding the extra fabric around her finger and releasing it, again and again.

When she did finally speak, she started slowly, as if unsure if she should continue. "I don't know if I should be discussing Lady Swindon's business, even though she is gone now..."

A distant clock ticking was the only sound in the room as they waited for her to finish.

"It isn't proper." Agnes knitted her brow together. "The first rule of service is to protect the family you work for, not slander them, not give away all their secrets. Everyone has secrets, don't they? It doesn't mean that they are killed for them. Perhaps it really was an accident. Perhaps she was just ill. It isn't as though we know every disease that exists. Maybe it was something she picked up travelling, or in London. I understand the doctor didn't think it was Spanish Flu, but it could have been anything...."

Lillie watched her face become more and more anxious as she spoke.

"True," she responded. Agnes seemed to relax slightly at her agreement. "But her symptoms were very odd indeed. Certainly odd for any disease that we know of." Lillie decided to switch tactics. "Tell me, what was your impression of Lord Swindon?"

"Oh, I don't know. He was...that is, he used to be very pleasant."

"Go on."

"Well about a year or so ago, I noticed a change in him. I

thought it had to do with the end of the war. Sometimes people find their way during times of war. Some business does well, doesn't it? His business certainly did. But he seemed to change overnight. He became sharp tongued, not only with the downstairs staff, but also with his family," she said, then cut off abruptly.

"Tell me more about that. Was there tension between Lord and Lady Swindon particularly?"

"Oh, I don't know..."

"Except I think you *do* know, Agnes. I think a lady's maid is in a very privileged position to know more than most would."

"I suppose so."

"Was there some reason separate from what you have just said about the war? Something personal between them causing this angst?"

Agnes was beginning to look worn down, her previously stony suit of armour starting to crack. Lillie thought she wanted to tell someone, and hoped it would be them. They waited.

"There was something. I know it bothered her. She was sad sometimes. Like something was lost, long ago. Never mind, I'm not making any sense."

"You are, go on," Lillie urged.

"She spoke once of someone she loved—this is going back years, to when she was young. Of course I am sure it has nothing to do with her death. People don't die of sadness, now do they?"

"I don't think that is the case here, no."

"Anyway, some time back, around the end of the war, she took a trip for a few days, by herself. She didn't ask me to accompany her, which was odd. I always went with her when she traveled. Instead she let me have a few days off. She was kind like that. When she returned, everything in the house changed. It was different."

"Different in what way?" Harry asked, intrigued.

"Colder. Is that a way to describe a house, or the people in it? Cold? Lord Swindon seemed angry and removed. Spent much of his time in his library or in London. Eventually he seemed to soften a little. Even threw her an enormous party for her birthday, *and* bought her that necklace. It was the talk of the village. That night she wore the most ravishing dress—I'll never forget it—it had a velvet bodice laced with crystal beads, and they glinted when the candlelight caught them. Honestly, I imagined her as I would a queen." Her eyes had taken on a faraway look. "She got sick shortly after but at least they had that wonderful party. By the time she died he was by her side again. I have no doubt he loved her very much. He was devastated after she passed."

"Do you know where Lady Swindon went on that trip by herself?"

"No. I don't. But wherever it was, it certainly changed things..."

"WELL, THAT WAS ENLIGHTENING," Harry mused quietly as they left Agnes and began their journey back to Claridge's.

Lillie scanned the street quickly for the man she thought she had spied before their meeting but didn't find him lurking about. She was probably imagining things. "It was, yes. Where do you think Lady Swindon went on that secret trip?"

"I wish I knew. It is curious. Tell me, do you think Lord Swindon should be a suspect? Obviously he wasn't happy in the year leading up to her death. Something had happened between them. And, thanks to my mother's idle gossip, we know she once had a dalliance with an Irish man, and while she was married, no less. Perhaps it is a simple case of a man scorned."

"I don't disagree with you, but he did seem to love her. Very much."

"Yes, but did she love *him*? That is the real question."

"Do you think we should attempt to speak with Lord Swindon again? Our last visit didn't really bring out the best in him." Lillie rubbed the scar on her forehead and stared out the window of the cab as they rounded Hyde Park corner and circumvented Apsley House, its golden Georgian facade turning a burnt pink with the setting sun.

"He was as tight lipped as the Mona Lisa. Yes, we should probably get in touch with him. But first I want to find out where Lady Swindon went on her trip and why is it such a secret."

"A tall order," Lillie replied. "And here is another one—I think we are going to need disgraced Constable Worley in London to help us get a visual on the man who bribed him. We need to know who he is or who he is working for."

"You're right." Harry was quiet for a minute, perhaps pondering the same point she was: how were they going to actually find the man who did the bribing, and where would that take them? On whose doorstep would they come knocking?

"I suppose we could send word to him. I'll write a letter when we get back to the hotel—although how we will flush out this criminal, I've no idea."

"Let's start with getting Worley here if we can, it'll cost us but it may well be worth it. Then we can let ourselves get bogged down in specifics," Lillie added. She didn't want to admit that the loosely floating pieces of the case were beginning to bother her. She craved some sense of order, or at least a connection.

"Do you think Lady Swindon was still in touch with the Irish chap she had an affair with thirty years ago?" Harry had a puzzled look on his face.

"No idea. Would you still be in touch with a long-lost love of yours?" Immediately she regretted the words, thinking of Jack. Her eyes welled up with tears. And then it struck her—of *course* she would be in touch with an old love if she could be. Immediately she stopped doubting that Lady Swindon would have done exactly the same thing. The Irishman could be the key to this whole thing. Lillie turned to look at Harry square on.

Harry knew what she was thinking, she could tell from his face.

They both said it at the same time. "Yes."

Harry nodded and decided to address the elephant in the room. He said gently, "Perhaps this...this grief, is your cross in life. It is the thing that can keep you sidelined—whittling away your life in a New York drawing room—if you let it. Jack wouldn't have wanted that for you, you must know that." It was the first time Harry had spoken his name out loud in her presence. "Granted, he would have me skinned alive if he knew we were running around England trying to solve a murder, but still, he knew you were capable of great things. A truly modern woman."

Lillie smiled. "Thank you, Harry. If I think about it logically, I know there must be more than one person out there, for me I mean, or for anyone. The problem is, I can't make my heart feel it."

"Not enough time has passed, my dear. There will never be another Jack, but there will be someone else for you. Not now, of course, but one day." He patted her hand in assurance.

"I am not sure I care enough to look for one. I am fine on my own. But enough about me. What about you?"

"What about me?" Harry asked.

"Is there anyone special you might be thinking of? Besides Beatrice, of course."

"Bite your tongue, you rotten girl."

"I have noticed your manners improve whenever Primrose is in your vicinity."

"I haven't the faintest idea what you are talking about." Harry felt his face flush.

"You really are the most appalling liar. Did boarding school teach you nothing?" The car pulled up in front of the magnificent facade of Claridges. The bellman opened the door with a small bow, breaking the conversation.

"Oh, look. Here we are, back at the hotel." Harry jumped out and paid the driver, glad for the diversion.

12

LILLIE

"**W**ORLEY IS MISSING," Harry stated matter-of-factly, alternating between sipping his coffee and reading the morning post in the well-appointed breakfast room of Claridges Hotel. It had been three days since their meeting with Agnes and Harry's subsequent sending word to Rumple to request Worley's presence in London. Harry continued to scan the letter he was holding, flipping back and forth between the pages. Lillie noticed that whoever had written it must have had quite a lot to say—the writing was crammed and there were at least four pages of it.

Primrose, fork raised halfway to her mouth, put it back down on her plate. "Dead?" she inquired, her astonished face fearful.

Harry put the letter he was reading down on the table. "It doesn't appear that way. It seems Rumple had the foresight to have him followed, and, upon receiving word that we had requested his company in London, he hopped on his criminally-obtained Triumph motorcycle and vanished. Rumple's spy tailed him to the edge of Iffley, but lost sight of him once he circumvented the site of the old watermill."

Swallowing a bite of strawberry, Lillie said, "I'm not surprised. Jeremy Winston called me this morning and apparently my first two columns have caused quite a stir."

"You never said! How so?" Primrose asked.

"Let's just say a few feathers have been ruffled. The newspaper office was stormed by the police yesterday afternoon—a show of blustering force to let us know they don't appreciate our naming their incompetence, no doubt. But really, what could they expect that action to achieve? I suppose they want Jeremy to be the sacrificial lamb. They are threatening to stop the presses and arrest staffers."

"That is terrible! Are you sure this is all worth it? It sounds a great deal more serious than a few ruffled feathers." Primrose pushed her plate aside, apparently having lost her appetite.

"Absolutely worth it. This just means we have been right all along to suspect *Something is rotten in the state of Denmark.* And anyway, Jeremy has a string of vicious and sharp-toothed legal advisors. The Constabulary has no idea what it has bitten off in the form of a seasoned newspaper man."

"I just despise confrontation," Primrose said, hunching her shoulders and shrinking into her seat.

"No one likes it, but sometimes it's necessary."

Harry nodded. "I forgot to mention. Did you know Lord Swindon is a member of the Athenaeum club?"

"Really? And do you think perhaps he may have been stuffing some money in their stationery and bribing a police officer?" Lillie asked, searching for another strawberry.

"We really don't have anything to tie him to Worley's bribe —countless wealthy men are members of the Athenaeum club."

"Hmm," Lillie said, chewing. *It must cost a small fortune to import strawberries at this time of year,* she thought. "Maybe not, but, along with his behaviour, it should be marked as suspicious."

Primrose looked thoughtful. "Not to put my nose in, but don't you think if Lady Swindon was having an affair, for *decades,* that she would have confided in someone about it?"

"It's possible," Lillie replied.

"Perhaps she had a close friend whom she told? I would certainly tell you, Lillie, if I was having a decades-old love affair with a dashing man from my youth."

Lillie noticed Harry startle. Probably the thought of Primrose having an affair with anyone but him drove him mad.

"What shall we do today, ladies?" he chimed in quickly, attempting to change the subject. Lillie couldn't believe how transparent he was being and how oblivious Primrose was for not noticing.

"I was actually hoping to take a few hours to myself and get some shopping done. I haven't brought enough things with me and I want to see if I can pick up some essentials at the shops," Lillie said. She suddenly felt the distinct sensation they were being watched, and felt goosebumps break out on her skin.

"Shall I join you?" Primrose asked.

"You may if you like, although I can't promise it will be very exciting. Perhaps we can have tea somewhere very posh when we are finished?"

Primrose nodded. "Harry, will you join us?"

"Heavens no. I despise shopping."

"I haven't really thought about where we should go, any suggestions?" Lillie said distractedly as she scanned the dining room for whoever had given her the creepy sensation. She thought she caught a glimpse of the same man she had noticed in front of Agnes's townhouse. She hadn't noticed him when he'd sat down—if it were him—because he hadn't been wearing the same green tweed overcoat as before.

Now she kept one eye on the people milling about the reception desk as she tried to locate him—the chair he had been occupying was disappointingly empty. The whole thing was probably just a ridiculous coincidence anyway. Surely people must bump into the same person from time to time, even in a city as large and teeming as London. It was just statistics.

"Selfridges is the hot place, so I hear." Harry said, dabbing at the sides of his mouth with his napkin. "Although I rarely venture farther than Jermyn Street for my clothing." He cleared his throat mock importantly.

"You are a snob, Harry. Selfridges it is then, for us commoners," Lillie teased. She focused her attention back on her companions and attempted to shake off the eerie feeling that they were being watched.

"When do you expect your sister to arrive in London?" Harry asked, brushing imaginary crumbs off his impeccably pressed trousers, oblivious to Lillie's distraction.

"She should be here the day after tomorrow. I am looking forward to seeing her, it surprises me how much I have missed her. How long do you think we will be staying in London?"

A sharply dressed waiter arrived at the table to refill their coffee cups.

"As long as it takes, I should think. Although I must admit the city is beginning to get under my skin," Harry said. "As T.S. Eliot so aptly put it: *Unreal city, under the brown fog of a winter dawn.*"

"The city is under your skin or your mother is under your skin?" Lillie asked, raising her eyebrows at him.

"You have a point, my dear girl. Now you two had better get on if you are to be back in time for supper."

"Primrose, shall we meet in the lobby in a half hour? I just want to put the finishing touches on my column and have it in the post today for Jeremy."

"What have you written?" Harry asked. "We've hardly found out anything that makes for riveting reading, have we? After all, one can hardly report that Lady's Swindon's maid confirmed she has been pining for decades over a long-lost love." Harry picked up a piece of bacon and nibbled on it thoughtfully.

"I can, actually, and I intend to. Flushing out this other man will require that I do report on the affair—I can cloak it somewhat by saying it is rumour or gossip, but I still need to write about it," Lillie said, looking determinedly at Harry.

"Oh dear, that will be scandalous." Harry said, wincing and carefully wiping bacon grease off of his fingers.

"You didn't bring me here to be a wallflower, Harry. And don't forget, we still don't understand exactly what happened medically with Lady Swindon. We haven't learned anything further on the score of poisoning, nor ascertained whether or not she had any enemies. She certainly doesn't seem to have any, even despite her dalliances. But that was so long ago it hardly seems relevant now. Unless..." Lillie didn't finish.

"Unless she had a child by way of that dalliance," Primrose finished for her.

"That would be an enormous reveal, granted, but how can we possibly prove that now? And what of the police investigation, or lack of it?" Lillie frowned. "There are so many loose ends and hardly any explanations. I fear you may have brought me all this way for nothing, Harry. As the days go by I wonder whether or not we will ever be any the wiser on this case."

"Fear not, I haven't resigned myself to ignorant bliss quite yet. Someone paid off a police constable to not investigate the death. Most certainly this means there *was* a murder and Lady Swindon didn't eat lettuce accidentally grown in cyanide. Now, away with you both. Clean out those shops!"

"I admire your perseverance in the face of adversity. And to think I always thought you...oh, never mind," Lillie said, stifling a little laugh.

"Frivolous? Vacant? Silly, even?" Harry winked at her.

"I was going to say something else entirely—anemic,

perhaps?" She wished she hadn't said it, but he could be a bit of a sapless beautillion at times—albeit a loveable one.

"Oh, how very rude. I certainly dislike having having my character questioned at such an early hour. Now go! I can't relax under these conditions—you nattering at me incessantly."

THE CARVED, neo-classical columns of Selfridges Department Store towered over Oxford Street, casting a broken shadow on the early morning shoppers. Throngs of pleased onlookers, their breath frozen in cold and anticipation of what the day's revelation would be, huddled on the sidewalk while great, billowing, gauze curtains were ceremoniously raised to reveal multiple window displays—each wallpapered and decorated overnight with the glitz and pomp so anxiously awaited and adored. Through the glass doors, salespeople buzzed around their displays like bees on a hive, a blur of pale pink lipstick, coiffed hair and rustling skirts. Their polished shoes clacked on the marble floors like the sound of typewriter keys.

"Oh my!" Primrose gasped, stopping suddenly as she came through the main doors. She gazed around the first floor, seemingly intoxicated by the hundreds of glittering bottles, a sea of silk accessories, and a garden of scent. "I haven't ever seen such a store!"

Lillie laughed. "We need to get you to the city more often. It *is* remarkable, I admit— although what with having R.H. Macy and Gimbels back in America, I am not as quite as starstruck as you are right now. Come, let's check out the ladies' fashions department." Lillie gently took her arm and steered her away from the main entrance, deep into the heart of the building.

They spent the better part of the morning perusing the various sections of the store and by lunchtime Lillie's arms were laden with armloads of bags and both had hungry stomachs. They made their way to the Palm Court restaurant and were shown to a table near the window. Enroute they passed a group of four men having lunch, one of whom was Lord Swindon.

"Should I go over and say hello?" Lillie asked Primrose as they took their seats.

"Based on what you said about your last visit, perhaps you should pretend you didn't see him."

"Might be better, yes. Do you see that other man he is with? The one with the navy and red tie?" Primrose craned her neck around to scan the restaurant. "Don't be too obvious..." Lillie warned.

Primrose turned her attention back to Lillie.

"Yes, do you know him?"

"If I am not mistaken, I think I met him once, months ago, at my sister's house in Manhattan. Mr. Fitz...something-or-other, I can't remember. I don't think I would have given him a second glance now if it weren't for his tie."

Primrose did another subtle sweep of the restaurant. "Eton," she stated succinctly, looking back at Lillie.

"That's right, you do know your school colours."

"I may not be upper class, but I am English."

"Primrose, darling, you have more class in your pinky finger than anyone in Debrett's, I can assure you. How many grown men do you know who still wear their school ties?"

"You would be surprised...but I agree, it isn't the norm," she replied.

"He really isn't the most attractive man, is he? Lord Swindon, I mean."

"Not really, which makes you wonder...."

"If the dashingly handsome Edgar is really his son?" Primrose said, raising her eyebrows.

"Exactly. Doesn't look a thing like him." Lillie watched the table, twirling her hair around her finger. Was it just a coincidence that she would meet a man and then see him again halfway across the world, dining with the husband of the subject of her murder investigation? There seemed to be too many coincidences going on in her life at the moment.

"That's it, then. I am going over there to say hello."

"I thought you weren't going to, oh dear," Primrose said, flustered. "Shall I come with you?" She made a show of pushing back her chair, looking as though it was the very last thing in the world she wanted to do.

Lillie shook her head and got up, placing her napkin on the table. "It's better I do this alone." She felt Primrose's eyes on her as she walked over to the men's table.

Four faces looked up at her as she approached. "Lord Swindon, hello. I was just dining with a friend and saw you across the restaurant," Lillie said, looking down at a startled Lord Swindon, who hastily stood up to greet her. "And Mr....I am terribly sorry—I have forgotten your name. But I know we met in New York a few months ago, at my sister's house?"

"Fitzherbert. And yes, of course, I remember now. What a surprise to see you here." The man stood up and gave Lillie a little bow of his head. He looked completely surprised, and more than a little perturbed. His watery eyes darted back and forth between her and Lord Swindon. The two other men at the table also stood up and Lillie glanced at them in fleeting acknowledgement. She didn't want to take her eyes off Fitzherbert's face.

"Mr. Fitzherbert and I met in New York briefly," Lillie explained to Lord Swindon in the politest voice she could muster. "How do you two know one another?"

"We, uh...." Lord Swindon began to answer, but was sharply cut off by Fitzherbert.

"Just business my dear, just business," he said in a sickly sweet, dismissive voice. Lillie was instantly annoyed.

She kept pressing. "Oh yes, and your business is...remind me again...gemstones or something or other?"

Fitzherbert stared coldly at her and didn't answer. Lord Swindon was beginning to look confused, alternating between looking at the two of them. He was seemingly trying to understand his business associate's hostility.

"Red ones, weren't they?" Lillie knew she should tread carefully.

Still he didn't answer her.

"Didn't Lady Swindon have some of your gemstones in her collection?" She was taking stab in the dark as she remembered with vividity the necklace in Lady Swindon's room at Wrenhaven. Lord Swindon looked surprised at this—although whether it was surprise at her knowing this, or surprise at her inappropriateness, Lillie couldn't be sure.

The continued silence was laden with tension. Lillie let it linger for as long as she could stand it.

"Please don't let me disturb your luncheon. I just wanted to say hello." She smiled and returned to her table.

When she sat back down, Primrose leaned in so they wouldn't be overheard. "Well?"

"Well, *that* was uncomfortable. I don't think anyone was happy to see me. I can understand that response from Lord Swindon, but that Fitzherbert fellow, the one I met in New York, was not particularly fond of the intrusion. He is in the gemstone business, incidentally—and, if I remember correctly, Lady Swindon had an enormous necklace with one of his stones."

"Well, that could fit. It seems she was very fond of gemstones. Obviously Lord Swindon purchased them from that man, or did when his wife was alive."

"Perhaps, yes. But why the awkwardness when I showed up?"

"I have no idea, but imagine how much more awkward it

would have been had your column been published revealing Lady Swindon's affair. Luckily it was today that you ran into him and not tomorrow after the papers hit the news stands!"

"Well, never mind. Let's enjoy our lunch," Lillie said, with a lightheartedness she didn't feel.

There was something strange about Fitzherbert, of that much she was sure. Whether or not she was imagining his veiled hostility there was something he was hiding—even more disturbing was his past presence in her sister's home. All at once, the Swindon case and her own family were beginning to feel too close to one another for her own comfort.

13

LILLIE

"STRANGE HOW? CAN YOU BE just a little more precise?"

They were talking about Fitzherbert again that evening as Harry was attempting to hail a taxi outside Covent Garden. It had begun to rain; Lillie pulled her coat around her and held her purse over her head. The two of them had just finished eating a light supper at Rules and were trying to get back to their hotel. Primrose, having complained that her feet were sore from shopping, was back at Claridge's to peruse the classifieds. Lillie could tell that this had sent Harry into a silent tailspin, perhaps at the thought of her moving to London permanently. Lillie wished she was also curled up there beside a crackling fire, rather than freezing out here on a wet sidewalk with Harry.

"He is—oh, I don't know—slippery."

"As in criminal? Is that what you mean? Oh, damnation!" Harry swore in exasperation as another full taxi passed him by.

"Shouldn't we just start walking? It'll be midnight before we get one." The street was crowded with evening theatregoers and their chances of finding a car was diminishing exponentially as the Drury Lane spilled its sharply dressed patrons onto the sidewalk along with them.

Lillie ducked under an eave and blew on her wet hands to try and warm them. She watched crowds of people intermingle, not seemingly concerned with either the rain or the time, and idly listened to snippets of their critiques of that night's performance of Il Trovatore, their tones and gestures often as dramatic as the operatic characters she imagined had been on stage tonight. *Terribly muddled plot...I could hardly understand...backstory, what backstory?...did you see that costume?...a rising star, to be sure...and the voice of a songbird...did you see the other performance at...apparently the understudy is rather fond of his whiskey...*

She noticed a man across the street, partially obscured by the shadows of a streetlamp. At first she thought he was watching the theatre-goers, but she quickly realized that as they moved on, his eyes did not. He wasn't close enough for her to make out his face. Perhaps he was interested in Harry's excited display of leaping around in the rain attempting to get noticed by a driver, which admittedly was entertaining. But as the minutes ticked by and he didn't move, Lillie began to suspect that it was the same man she had seen before at Agnes's and then again in the hotel lobby that morning. It was too dark to see the colour of his coat, so she couldn't be sure, but one thing was certain: she was fed up with wondering about an unknown man who appeared to be following her all over London. This was no coincidence.

Waiting until his attention was back on Harry, she shot out into the street, hoping she was unobserved for the moment, and within seconds was standing behind him in the shadow of an unlit alley. Her heart pounded in her chest, from the exertion or nervousness, she didn't know. She had the perfect vantage point to observe the man, but she knew she wouldn't go unnoticed for long. He was wearing the tweed coat she had spotted before, the giveaway woven yellow strand now obvious from close quarters. He appeared to be about sixty years old, with a still-thick head of steely iron-grey hair that curled where it met his collar. In profile, he had strong facial features: a sharp nose and a blunt chin with high cheekbones. He was tall, and lean, with none of the stoutness many men acquire throughout the years, and Lillie assumed he did physical work—a farmer perhaps, or a miner?

He was looking for her now, or so she thought, taking his attention off of Harry and scouring the sidewalk across the street with his roaming eyes. For a moment Lillie prayed Harry wouldn't get a taxi, or he too would realize she was no longer there. The man stepped forward, and began to pace, obviously thinking she had begun walking and wanting to keep up. He looked anxious, and frustrated, and she figured now was as good a time as any to confront him.

"Are you looking for me?" Lillie steadied her voice as best she could.

The man whirled around, startled, and faced her. His dark eyes were wide with surprise and Lillie wondered briefly if she had made the right choice, confronting him on her own.

"I...I..." He grasped for words.

"Who are you?" Lillie demanded. "And why have you been following me?" Across the street Harry had stopped his antics and had noticed them. He hesitantly took a few steps into the street, looking both ways for cars, and then began to jog towards them.

"Aye, I have been. Please, I don't mean any harm, not to you, or your friends. My name is Blackie McGurrin, and I..." Here he hesitated. "I knew Ellie Swindon."

His Irish accent was broad and lilting. Lillie raised an eyebrow, *Ellie*. That sounded rather...affectionate. Could this be the long lost love of Lady Swindon's life? Even with his advancing years, Lillie could understand the attraction. His face was strong, with sharp, dark eyes that glistened now by the light of the moon. He had a furrowed brow, permanently concerned or unsure, she couldn't tell which. His clothes, on close inspection, were good quality but worn in the way a pair of shoes would be, still handsome but a little scuffed around the toes. Overall, he was a pleasant-looking man, the years having done little to detract from his quiet masculinity. By now, Harry had arrived at her side out of breath, and had the good sense not to say a word.

She supposed she had to introduce him. "Mr. McGurrin, this is my friend Harry Green, but I suppose you know that already." Harry remained silent as Blackie nodded at him.

"Well!" She breathed life into the word. "Since we all know each other then, how about we get a cup of coffee and you, Mr. McGurrin, can tell us how you knew Lady Swindon."

At precisely that moment, a large black cab stopped in front of them, delivering its carload of gregarious passengers in a waft of nauseating perfume.

Harry finally found his words. "What are the odds?"

BACK AT THE HOTEL, the bartender, having let his wait staff go home for the evening, brought three large whiskeys over to the polished table himself and carefully set them, along with a plate of assorted sandwiches, gently down in front of them.

"Room 21, Green, thank you," Harry said, nodding to him.

Lillie regretfully noticed the cup of coffee had been disregarded. "And a cup of coffee for me please," she requested, scowling at Harry and pushing her glass towards him.

"Yes, madam. I shall assign the bill accordingly, sir. Would you like an additional round before I close for the evening? There's no rush—you may sit here all night if you wish."

"Please." Harry didn't look at Lillie or Blackie for confirmation on the issue. "And would you kindly stoke up that fire before you go? Terribly chilly evening."

The barman nodded at Harry and took his leave.

"Well, that is better," Harry, exhaling, sank into his dark green leather chair and took a large sip of whiskey.

"It does warm the insides," Blackie said, nodding and doing the same.

"So you are the Irishman we have been hearing about," Lillie said.

While she wasn't skeptical of his identity, she was very concerned about why he had followed them, not choosing to reveal himself. It was hardly behaviour befitting an innocent man.

"Well, lass, I am not sure what you have heard, but I did know Ellie, yes. I heard about her death"—here he paused to wipe at his eyes—"and then about you. I read your column, and I came here to help. If I can, that is."

Lillie studied his face. *Were the tears real?* she wondered. She figured the best way to expose whether he was genuine or not was to get him talking. "Tell me about how you and Lady Swindon met."

He paused, obviously weighing how to proceed. "I am not really one for reminiscing...memories, you see, are the province of old women and priests. And talking about her won't bring her back." His voice was soft and full of emotion but there was an edge to it as well.

"Please, if you don't tell us about her history, we will have to find someone else who will."

Blackie seemed to consider this, remaining silent, while he sipped his whiskey and stared into the fire. Eventually he said, "I don't know much about her history."

"Is that so?" Lillie asked skeptically. "And yet you choose to follow me all over this city to see what I am up to with regards to her case. Seems a little odd for someone who doesn't really know Lady Swindon."

"I liked her. That's all. She used to spend summers visiting her uncle's estate in Kilkenny; I've known her since she was a girl but seeing someone a few weeks a year doesn't mean you really get to know them." He spoke as though she were still alive.

"What did the two of you do when she would visit? Did you go places, meet people?" Lillie wasn't sure now whether this *was*, in fact, the man Lady Swindon was suspected of having an affair with. Other than the earlier emotion he had had in his voice, he was acting fairly nonchalant about the whole thing. She wondered if this was intentional.

"Sometimes. But the estate wasn't near anything much, the nearest town was twenty miles away, so we often made our own entertainment. We used to take this old row boat out..." he smiled, then paused, "...never mind, it isn't important."

Lillie let it lapse and took a different tack. "Why were you on the estate? Did your family live there?"

"My father was the blacksmith, we had a small cottage near the stables."

"I see, and did you keep in touch in recent years?"

The man didn't answer, choosing instead to stare into his whiskey glass as though the answer could be found hidden in the swirls of amber. Eventually, he gave a sigh and looked up. "No, we didn't."

"When was the last time you spoke to her?"

"I really can't remember...I had better be going, it's late." Blackie got up and thanked Harry for the drink.

"But we aren't finished...I need to know more," Lillie was up now too and she looked to Harry for help.

"I'm afraid we are finished, there isn't anything else to say anymore—she's dead." He was buttoning up his coat quickly and began to make for the lobby.

"But...yes, of course she is dead but we need to know why! Mr. McGurrin..." Lillie was trailing behind him now and marvelled at the length of his stride as he crossed the lobby in a few long steps. The street was quiet as they spilled outside into the darkness. Lillie rubbed at her bare arms regretting leaving her coat on her chair.

Blackie looked down at her, seemingly perplexed that she had followed him. "Go inside. There isn't anything I can tell you that will help with the investigation. I only came out of respect."

"That isn't entirely true and you know it. What are you hiding?"

"Goodnight, Miss Mead. And good luck."

His retreating back was swallowed up in the darkness.

14

LILLIE

THE SIDEWALK WAS STILL WET from the overnight deluge, and Lillie gave her undivided attention to where she was placing her feet in the midst of an extensive network of pooling water. Her sister would be annoyed with her for being late if she slowed down, but it would be a miserably long day if she was to suffer through it with wet shoes. It was Penny's first day in London and she was hardly the kind of sister who was flexible on arrival time or amenable to sloppy dress.

Lillie's walk from Mayfair to Penny and Floyd's Belgravia hotel, although rushed, gave her time to reflect on their evening with Blackie McGurrin. She noticed she wasn't being followed and supposed that had come to an end now that the Irishman had revealed himself. Their case was, at the moment, a harried mess of loose threads: Lord Swindon and his strange behaviour; Blackie McGurrin and his lack of transparency; and the source of Constable Worley's bribe still anonymous and at large. She was frustrated with herself for letting Blackie walk out of the hotel bar last night without discovering where he was staying or how long he planned to be in London. She also didn't really understand what he wanted. All finding him had done was muddy the water and put him squarely on their list of suspects.

The sun had just started to peek through the clouds as Lillie arrived, ten minutes late, at the entrance of the Grand Hotel Belgravia. She glanced up at the sky and reflected how its hesitant blue overshadowed by an ominous dark-grey horizon precisely mirrored her own thoughts today.

The lobby of Penny's hotel differed sharply from the cozy, understated elegance of Claridge's. This lobby was decorated with gilded paintings, polished marble, and fabulously obscene crystal chandeliers the size of draft horses. It was an American-owned hotel, and Lillie couldn't help but feel the obvious display of opulence was out of touch with England's own state of post-war affairs. The decor was seemingly oblivious to the hunger, disease, and unemployment right outside its front doors. How could her sister and Floyd, with their financial troubles, afford to stay here?

She spotted her sister sitting across the lobby, idly reading a magazine and tapping her perfectly clothed foot. Her attention was less on the magazine and more on the large clock behind the reception desk. *Here it goes*, thought Lillie as she rushed forward to greet her.

"Finally!" her sister exclaimed, jumping up to hug her. "I was starting to think you had forgotten me."

"Nonsense. How could I ever forget you? I walked from Mayfair and it took a little longer than I had anticipated." Lillie noticed her sister was wearing a new necklace of sparkling red gemstone drops, each encased in a pave of diamond melee.

They flopped down on the velvet divan sofa Penny had been reading on and Lillie peered down at her wet shoes, dismayed at her lack of navigational skills and surprised at how much mud they had picked up. She discreetly tucked them underneath the sofa, hoping her sister wouldn't notice.

"Floyd is just there," Penny pointed across to the concierge desk where her tall, handsome husband was animatedly discussing something with a confused looking man in a navy-blue-and-gold hotel uniform. Even the employee clothing was grandiose, Lillie noted. "He is trying to get some directions—he has a business meeting today and isn't sure exactly how to get there. Now, tell me, what should we do today?" Penny didn't wait for Lillie to answer. "I know! I would love to have tea in Hyde Park, is there a tea room there? Or in any park really, although it is hardly a good day for it. I am certain the clouds are going to open up again—what a dismal city London is in the winter. What is the name of that restaurant again, the one Papa used to take us to?"

Lillie finally was able to get a word in. "Wiltons."

"Of course, that's it. But it isn't a tea room, so let's try for somewhere else, shall we? And then shopping, I want to get some scent, and I need a dress for the Vanderbilt ball next month. I certainly don't want to look like I bought it in New York, after all."

Lillie's head was beginning to swim, her sister's energy was already beginning to exhaust her. She smiled patiently at her. "I am happy to do anything you like. It is just nice to spend time with you."

This was obviously the right response, as Penny beamed and reached forward to clasp her hand. "I have missed you so! The house isn't the same without you. When are you coming home?"

"Not for a while. I am working again—for the newspaper in Oxford. I am really enjoying it."

"Oh yes, Floyd mentioned that," Penny replied, brushing it off. "Now, should we get a taxi? I really don't think walking is a good idea in this weather. Where did I put my purse..." She began searching around the sofa in earnest.

Lillie was surprised and flattered.

"How did Floyd know I was working for the Oxford Daily Press?"

Finding her purse, Penny stood up. "I don't know. Why don't you ask him—here he comes now."

Floyd was striding towards them with an enormous smile on his face. He picked Lillie up in his huge arms and swung her around like a doll.

"Dearest Lillie! How delightful to see you. How is England treating you? Your sister is terribly downcast without you."

Back on the ground, Lillie smoothed her skirt and smiled up at him. "I am enjoying being back here—not London particularly, but England in general. Penny tells me you heard about the column I am writing for the newspaper."

"Oh did I..." Floyd said, looking around the lobby distractedly, then pulling a gold lighter and cigarette case out of his breast pocket. He offered her one and she shook her head. "Yes, I suppose I did hear that somewhere. And is it a temporary column, or will it be a regular fixture for the newspaper?" He held the cigarette between his lips and snapped the lighter.

"We will see how it goes. It's a crime column, as you know," she said.

"Crime?" That had gotten Penny's attention.

"Yes. I am reporting on what appears to be a murder investigation."

"Is that dangerous?" Penny inquired.

Lillie deliberately ignored the question. "Floyd, what business brings you to London?"

"Oh, a little of this and that..." he said non-committally, taking a long drag from his cigarette and exhaling away from them.

Lillie didn't understand how Penny and Floyd kept up such a lavish lifestyle if they had had to sell the horses and furniture back in New York, and looked to Penny in slight confusion.

"Floyd, tell Lillie what we are really doing here," Penny

admonished, reaching up to touch her necklace. "These little beauties..." she prompted him.

"Oh?" Lillie was intrigued.

"Well, we'll see. I am meeting with a company in that business anyway."

"You remember the gentleman at our dinner party in New York, don't you?" Penny asked. "Mr. Fitzherbert?"

Lillie nodded, reluctantly.

"Well we are here to tour his cutting and sorting lab. He is looking for investors for his coloured stone mine."

"Yes, well, it isn't all that...." Floyd's words seemed to be failing him and he simply shrugged the rest of his sentence.

"I actually saw him the other day, at Selfridges. The Fitzherbert fellow."

"Ah. How nice," Floyd replied absent-mindedly.

"Well, not particularly nice. He was lunching with the husband of the victim whose death I am reporting on."

"Probably old friends, London is actually quite a small place when it comes to old school chums," he said, then added, "You two really should get going—beware, Penny has an agenda the length of her arm for today."

Lillie gathered up her coat, said her goodbyes, and followed Penny to the exit.

LATER THAT SAME AFTERNOON, after an exhausting few hours taking Penny to the sights, smells, and tastes of London, the two sisters ended up back on the divan sofa in the Grand Hotel as the light began to fade from the sky. One would have thought Penny might have had some semblance of the geography of the city, having spent much of her youth along with Lillie and their parents in London, but it seemed she had a sense of direction akin to a blind man in a desert.

"Shall we have some tea?" Penny asked.

"No, I'd better not. I told Harry I would be back in time for supper, so I really should get on. And I am sure Floyd has plans for the two of you. Perhaps tomorrow you can come and meet Harry and Primrose at the hotel? Breakfast?"

"Yes, I would like that. Floyd has business dealings for the better part of the day, so it will be a good distraction. Let me ask the bellman to get you a car."

"No, no. I assure you I can hail a cab back to my hotel without any assistance. I am an adult, you know."

"Of course you are, but I just want to make sure you don't attempt to walk the park on your own, since it is obviously going to rain buckets. Just look at that sky. You always liked to come home soaking wet in New York—remember how you ruined that beautiful dress I bought you for your birthday? I told you silk couldn't get wet and still you insisted on walking. And it was a Doucet! Utterly destroyed."

"I'm fine." She paused. "But tell me, before I go, how long are you in town for? Harry wondered if you might want to come visit Oxford?"

"I'm not sure, I'll have to ask Floyd. But a visit to Oxford would be heavenly—it would be a nice change from..." Penny paused, "well, from the day to day. Things have been a little difficult since you left New York."

"I can imagine, and yet here you are in this grand hotel."

Penny cast her eyes downwards. "Yes, apparently Floyd has been able to recover some of his lost fortune, thankfully. This trip was meant to be a distraction from the mess of the last few months."

Lillie watched her sister carefully. Judging by her face, whatever had gone on since she left America wasn't entirely over. "Well, never mind," Lillie said with false bravado, "here you are in this wonderful city and that is all that matters. If Oxford is in the cards then I say terrific."

Penny smiled at her and Lillie clasped her hand briefly while she pulled on her coat and did up the buttons.

"I would like that."

"As would I. Harry's estate at Tynesmore is breathtaking and there are loads of things to see in Oxford—the Bodleian Libraries especially, one could get lost for days in them. It is quite a delightful town—I have half thought of settling down there myself one day. Perhaps buying a cottage with a garden and a gate that creaks..." she winked at her sister.

"Please don't, libraries or not, I would miss seeing you terribly. Now go, quickly, before the skies open up. There is already a line up for cabs."

15

HARRY

THAT AFTERNOON, HARRY, realizing his good fortune at having received word from Rumple that suspended Oxfordshire constable Bruce Worley was holed up in the East End, arrived at a dilapidated bed-sit on Butler Street unannounced. The air was thick with coal dust and the creeping damp diffused itself throughout the filthy streets leaving a slick, toxic slime in its wake. He shuddered, feeling thankful he had worn his warmest coat and homesick for Tynesmore and the clean air of Oxford.

He glanced up at the three story facade, its dark grimy windows deadened eyes watching over a dismal landscape, and rapped on the door. He hoped Worley was in; the less time he spent in this area of London the better. He thought optimistically about what they would have for dinner at Claridge's when Lillie returned from her visit with her sister.

A couple of filthy-faced children, their moth-eaten clothes doing little to shield them from the cold, observed him from across the street. They slowly, hesitantly, made their way towards him. Harry reached into his pocket and had a pound for each of them before they reached his side. Astonished at their newfound fortune, they beamed up at him and hurried away.

The door was answered by a tired, underweight woman with a curved spine and a faded, paisley dress. She led him up a narrow, creaking staircase and along a slope-ceilinged hallway before stopping in front of a short, wooden door. She rapped loudly, then departed. It was opened by an unshaven Worley, wearing only his trousers, suspenders, and a mottled grey undershirt. Harry thought the man would have been surprised to see him, but if he were, there was no hint of it on his face.

He motioned for Harry to come in, which he did, glancing around a room that was as dismal on the inside as the house was on the outside. A threadbare rug, an uninviting iron bed, a stained wash basin and a small crooked table were the extent of the decor. Worley pulled out a chair for Harry, which creaked like kindling as he sat and, still without speaking, handed him a folded newspaper.

"What am I looking at?" They had clearly dispensed with any pleasantries.

Worley pointed at a picture on the front page. Harry studied the grainy photograph—a man with rounded features, a receding hairline, bright eyes, and a vaguely startled expression stared back at him. He glanced at the headline: "Man Dies After Suspicious Fall From London Bridge." He quickly skimmed the article and then looked at Worley, waiting for him to explain.

"This is him—the man who bribed me at the racetrack."

"Hang on—is this the reason you have arrived here in London out of the blue?" Harry held up the newspaper. "Murder or suicide? The article doesn't say, although I suppose one hardly falls off a bridge accidentally."

Worley raised his eyebrows.

"Scotland Yard says his name was Hewitt Darcy," Harry considered the paper again, looking for anything he might have missed. "Are you sure this is the same man? It isn't the clearest photo."

Worley nodded. "I never forget a face."

"Does that name mean anything to you?"

"Not a thing. It never came up in the investigation, if that is what you mean."

Harry stood up from the rickety table and put the paper down. "Right, so why *are* you here?" He wasn't going to beat around the bush.

"Crisis of conscience, I suppose," Worley said, and coughed, the low-lying East End pollution clearly bothering him. "I thought perhaps you could use my help."

"Who do you think killed this bloke?"

A fit of coughing ensued that seemed would never stop. "Whoever pushed this Darcy fellow off that bridge," Worley answered, wiping his mouth with a handkerchief, "is almost certainly the man we are looking for. Darcy must have been a patsy."

"So, our next move is?"

"I should think a visit to Scotland Yard."

"But won't that discredit you? The fact you allowed yourself to be bribed? You will never get back on the force."

"The damage has already been done. I have little left to lose."

"Right, tomorrow then. It's getting too late now and I need to meet with the girls. In the meantime, pack your things— you're coming with me. I don't want to lose track of you."

Worley looked confused. "Where are we going?"

"Somewhere a great deal more comfortable than here." Harry stood up, thankful his chair had held, and made his way to the door.

16

LILLIE

MAKING HER WAY OUT OF THE Grand Hotel Lobby and outside, Lillie realized Penny was right —the sky *was* dark and threatening rain. A frigid gust of air rattled the yellow-and-white awning of the hotel, its updraft tossing leaves into air and swirling them about as a river would a current. Disappointingly, there were no taxis in front of the hotel.

A doorman, rubbing his gloved hands together to warm them, asked, "Miss? Are you wanting a taxi?"

"I was, yes, but I don't see any about."

"No, we are having a long wait for them today—at least half an hour. If you would like to have a seat in the lobby, I can come get you when one arrives."

She didn't have the time, and Harry would be annoyed if she was late for dinner. It would be faster to make her way on foot. "I should think I will just walk after all. I haven't too far to go, and with any luck the rain will hold off."

The doorman tipped his hat. "As you wish, Miss. Although I think if you don't hurry, you may get wet."

Lillie set off across the street and through the gates into

Hyde Park, intending to cut through on the way back to Claridge's. She picked up her pace, fearing not just the rain, but also the falling darkness. She had known the park well in her younger days, but it had been years since she had last been here. She certainly didn't know it well enough now to navigate without light. The clouds had hurried most of the public off, and those that were still there were rushing to their destinations in much the same way she was. Gusts of wind rattled trees, their branches leaning and trunks squeaking. It blew through her clothing as though she had none on, lashing at her skin and whipping her skirt around her legs as she walked.

Lillie rounded a bend in the path and crossed through a particularly empty and wooded area of the park. It seemed at once darker. For a moment, she thought she heard footsteps behind her. She shivered and glanced back, but could see no one.

She increased her pace, now regretting that she had decided to walk. It was colder than she had thought, and she pulled her coat tighter with little effect. It began to rain and she felt the droplets hitting her hair. She had forgotten to wear a hat today, and it wasn't long before she felt the rain on her nose and cheeks.

The path narrowed as it negotiated winter-bare shrubbery long in need of trimming, their skeletal branches pulling at her coat as she passed, plucking and holding on, then releasing with a swish and a snap. She stepped off of the path to avoid a puddle blocking her way, and immediately regretted it as her shoes filled with mud from the sodden grass.

She suddenly felt very vulnerable out in the park in the rain and cold. *What was I thinking?* She should have waited in the warmth of the lobby for a taxi instead of being so willful and impatient. It would serve her right to show up at Claridge's soaking wet, her clothes ruined, and the onslaught of a cold a certainty.

There was a crack of thunder overhead and Lillie braced herself against another gust of wind. Suddenly, she heard a rustle of leaves on the path behind her and turned to see a figure following her. A man, dressed in a dark hat and a wrinkled oilcloth coat, his face concealed by an upturned collar, was matching her pace step-for-step. A feeling of dread enveloped her body and she knew, instantly and instinctually, that she was in grave danger. A chill rushed down her spine, her head cleared, and everything around her became hyper-focused, as though she was looking into the scope of a rifle. She was not just being followed—she was being pursued.

She began to run, her soaked shoes rubbing painfully against her feet, and she could hear him doing the same behind her. She sensed he was gaining on her even though she was going as fast as she could. She didn't care about the puddles or the pain in her throbbing feet now as she tried desperately to put distance between herself and the man behind her. Her heart beat madly in her chest and her breath caught raggedly as fear encircled her throat, suffocating and engulfing her every breath.

She had thought when Blackie had come forward that she was no longer being followed. That had obviously been a huge error in judgment on her part. She was being hunted like a fox, and the park she tore through now was as lonely as the winter moors. Ahead the path widened, opening into a clearing a hundred feet in front of her. If she could just get to it, there would be people there, or so she hoped. At the very least the man would be out in the open.

Eighty feet now. Her feet were beginning to numb as her legs furiously pumped like pistons. Fifty feet...thirty...if she could just reach it...her heart was hammering, her lungs burning...twenty feet...she stretched her stride as long as it could go...fifteen....

And then the man was upon her. She spun around in time

to see him raise an object above his head and bring it down on her. She ducked, but he was fast enough to catch her on the side of the temple. She heard a dull *thwack*. A ringing filled her ears; a dizzying nausea enveloped her. She fell to the ground, clutching her head and trying to maintain consciousness. Something warm and sticky trickled down her cheek—it took a minute to realize it was her own blood. Her vision began to fade to black as a dim outline of the man's foot rose and connected with her chin, throwing her onto her back. She heard the faintest cry, and realized it was her own as a curtain of darkness descended.

17

H E WAS RUNNING NOW, CALLING her name in a frenzied voice he didn't recognize. The sky was dark, but a sliver of the emerging moon allowed him to see her, slumped on the ground in front of him. Her attacker had run off at the sound of his voice, no doubt regretful he hadn't finished the job. Anger rose like bile inside his throat.

Finally reaching her, the man took off his overcoat and lay it over her. The grass beneath his feet was damp and cold, and he wished he had a blanket as well. The man noticed his hands were shaking. This was new for him. His colleagues often joked he had ice in his veins and perhaps had had his nerves surgically removed during the war. He prided himself in not being easily flustered, in not losing the slightest bit of control.

He crouched and felt her neck for a pulse, her skin thankfully warm—but he knew from experience that a dead body remained warm for a short time. The feel of her mesmerized him, transported him. She was breathing, thankfully, and he became aware his own breath had stopped. He willed himself to breathe in and out and focus on the next step. His training took over, all of it, years of it, and for this he was at once grateful. Gently, he wrapped her unconscious body in his coat. The feel of her skin, her clothes, the faintest scent of her underneath the earthen mud—he remembered it all. It was piercing and startling all at once, but he ignored it. There would be time for that later.

Removing his necktie, he made a bandage for her head and gently but firmly wrapped the silk around her. Calculating how to lift her without hurting her, he put his knees on the ground, very carefully getting his arms under her wrapped body. Pushing into the sodden earth, he managed to stand, cradling her in his arms.

Blood streamed through the necktie from the gash on her temple and mud mottled her long, auburn hair. She had been knocked around, in all probability with the intention to kill. He wouldn't be surprised if she had a few broken bones. All things considered, she was probably lucky to be unconscious at the moment.

He noticed with alarm that her hands were growing cold. Within only minutes of brisk walking, his coat was soaked with her blood. He knew head injuries bled the most and tried not to panic, going as quickly and carefully as he could. Across the grass he hurried, trying not to jostle her, but stumbling often. He met the footpath after what seemed like an eternity and from there the going became easier. But it all took so painstakingly long.

When he reached the road, he spotted an idle hackney carriage and made his way towards it. The driver, noticing his distress and the unconscious woman in his arms, leapt out and opened the door for them.

"Here, lay her here..." The driver motioned to the back seat.

The man laid her down and climbed in, giving the driver the quickest route to the hospital. For a fleeting moment, he wondered if he should take her to his flat and tend to her himself, but he couldn't take the chance.

The driver was quick and didn't dally. Ignoring all traffic regulations, he drove like a demon through the dark streets. The city whizzed by the windows, but the man was too distracted to notice as he carefully cradled her against his body to protect her from being abruptly thrust about in the corners. He watched her with intensity. If she were to wake, he wondered what he would say, how he would explain.

"Sorry, old chap," the driver called over his shoulder after one particularly sharp turn. "We're close now."

Within the minute, the cab pulled up in front of the hospital and the driver jumped out and ran into the building, presumably to fetch a doctor and a stretcher. The man thought idly that the driver must have been a soldier in the past, for he knew exactly what to do under pressure.

The man spoke softly to the unconscious woman beside him. "We are at the hospital. We are getting you help now." He didn't know what else to say, although there was so much. But it was enough for now. He doubted she could hear him anyway.

He looked up as the doors of the hospital were flung open and a stretcher was brought around the side of the car. As they loaded her, the man told the attending doctor everything he knew about her injuries. She was rushed away, and he hesitated, wondering if he should follow. It didn't take long to make his decision. He hurried to catch up.

A nurse stopped him at the doors to surgery and told him quietly that he could see her after she was evaluated. He turned on his heel, frustrated, and made his way to a waiting area where thankfully no one else was present. Here he paced for the better part of an hour before the nurse returned.

"She's coming around, but she'll need to stay here for treatment and rest. Would you like to see her now?"

"I—I'm—that is to say—I don't really know her, oddly enough." He felt transparent. "You see, I just found her in the park, unconscious, and she was injured...and, well, I brought her here."

"Do you know her name?"

How could he possibly say he did? Doing that would not only expose himself, but would open up a labyrinth they were all ill prepared for. He shook his head.

"Well," the nurse said, and sighed. "I suppose someone will eventually come looking for her. And by the looks of it, it will be a police matter."

"Before I go, did the doctor say anything about her head injury? It looked terribly bad."

"He seems to think she was lucky, if that means anything. Listen, let me get a pencil and take your name. Surely the police will want to interview you..." She turned to the nurse's station. The man took advantage of her distraction to disappear.

He left the hospital through a side door he had spotted on his way in, always marking alternative exit routes. Slipping into the alley, he made his way back to the main road and hailed a cab to take him back to the office. He needed to think carefully about his next move.

Climbing the stairs to the second floor of the red brick building, he found himself thinking about the many roads that had led him to his current life. He walked briskly down the corridor to his office, attempting to hide the blood on his shirt from a few late-night colleagues still at their desks. Completing their rabbit reports, no doubt. There were never enough hours in the day for agents to surveil and do their paperwork on targets. He closed the door and sank into his chair, looking down at his blood-stained clothes. He touched one of the spots. *Her* blood.

He reached across his walnut desk and retrieved a piece of nondescript paper and a pen, and began to write.

18

HARRY

THE LOBBY OF CLARIDGE'S HOTEL was surprisingly quiet, given the hour. Normally guests would have been coming and going to dinner, but owing to the time of year and the cold weather, it was hardly surprising that London wasn't its usual bustling self. From inside, Harry watched the doorman rubbing his hands together and hopping from one foot to the next between arriving guests. He wondered what was taking Lillie so long to return. Certainly shopping with her sister wouldn't have gone this long—it was nearly eight o'clock, and she had promised to be back by five.

Although Lillie was periodically late, it was unlike her not to send word. Harry wasn't sure if he should be annoyed or worried, and he attempted to push back a creeping sensation of the latter. He had had much to discuss with her over dinner, but owing to his grumbling stomach and her curious absence, he had decided to eat without her, assuming she had done the same. There was Worley and the dead man to discuss, of course, but Harry had also run into Lord Swindon that afternoon at the Athenaeum and Swindon had entirely snubbed him. His icy reception could have frozen the Sahara desert—

although, in reflection, Harry supposed he should hardly have been surprised, given Swindon's earlier resistance to their inquiries.

Harry watched the front door as a letter carrier rushed through it, bringing with him a cold gust of winter air. A moment later a front desk clerk stood in front of Harry's chair with the letter in hand.

Finally. *Silly girl, making him worry unnecessarily.*

"For you, sir, marked urgent."

Harry tore the envelope open with his index finger and read with incredulity.

Dear Sir:

It will interest you to know that an acquaintance of yours, a young woman, has been injured and is in the Royal London Hospital being treated. I found her unconscious in the Hyde Park a few hours ago and got her to hospital expediently. When I left the hospital the nurse reported she was regaining consciousness and that she was very lucky to be alive.

I urge you to make haste and get to her bedside. Moreover, I would suggest, or rather insist, that this young woman have a twenty-four-hour guard stationed outside her door until she recovers. I haven't the faintest doubt that her attacker meant to kill her, and once he knows that she is still alive, he will certainly attempt it again.

For your convenience, I have installed a watchman until you can make arrangements to have your own guard instated.

Regards.

The letter was unsigned.

Harry leapt out of his seat and ran to the house phone where he dialled Primrose's room.

"Come downstairs immediately! Lillie is in the hospital. We

have to go right now!" He hung up without waiting for a response and raced over to the doorman.

"Please, a taxi as quickly as possible—we haven't a moment to lose."

"Of course, sir." The doorman stepped off the sidewalk and waved his hands to summon a car.

Harry ran back inside the hotel to wait for Primrose, who at that moment emerged from the lift and ran towards him. Her scarf trailed behind her, her coat undone.

"What's happened? Harry?" She was breathless. Harry steered her towards the awaiting taxi.

"Here," he said, thrusting the letter into her hands. "Read as we drive." He leaned over the seat in front of them and spoke to the driver. "Royal London Hospital please, as quick as you can."

"Oh!" Primrose gasped as she read the letter. "Oh, dear Lord, poor poor Lillie."

Her eyes began to well up with tears and Harry said, rather more brusquely than he meant to, "Let's try not to be too emotional—it won't help matters. We must find out how badly she is injured and then we must find the culprit and mash him into a bloody pulp." He spat the last words out angrily.

"But...I don't understand," Primrose stammered. "Who wrote this letter?"

"I don't know. Obviously someone who knows who I am and that Lillie is known to me. It isn't important right now."

"But Harry, it is important—it is very important. Don't you see? This person knows you and knew exactly where Lillie was —in Hyde Park. How would he have known that if he hadn't been following her?"

"Well..." Harry paused, thinking. "He didn't hurt her, did he? He saved her. I don't understand all this, Primrose. We are onto something, obviously, or Lillie wouldn't have been attacked. Pity this person wasn't there before she was attacked —he might have stopped it. The thing is..." Harry glanced out the window, mulling it over. "I cannot understand who this person is or why he is watching us."

"Let's just get to the hospital and be there for Lillie. The rest of this will become clearer over time."

"I will send word tonight for Rumple to come to London immediately. I should have done it earlier. He certainly doesn't seem formidable when he plays the role of a gentrified manservant but trust me, the work he did during the war for the Defense of the Realm was—how shall I put it—somewhat unsavoury. In the meantime, we are going to need some security around the hospital room. My father can help us with that —I am sure he knows of a private security firm in London. I'll call him when we get there." Harry anxiously ran his hand through his hair.

"And we should get word to Lillie's sister Penny. She is staying at the Grand Hotel," Primrose said.

"Good, right. Of course." He added it to his mental to do list.

They fell into a fearful silence, thoughts swirling, as the taxi made its way through the dark streets towards the hospital.

19

LILLIE

THE HOSPITAL ROOM WAS AS DARK as coal. Only a sliver of light from the nurse's station sliced through its suffocating cloak.

Lillie's head throbbed and she reached up and touched it, the feel of gauze under her fingertips startling her. Her face was hot and she slipped her fingers down her cheeks, feeling stitches on her left temple. Her body ached when she tried to move, so she lay still, waiting, drifting in and out of a restless sleep.

She was dreaming. Jack was holding her hand, tickling her palm with his forefinger as they ran down a grassy slope to a glistening river, the way he always did. She laughed and squirmed under his touch. The spring sky was bright, but Jack motioned to the ominous storm clouds brewing. For a moment her happiness was infused with a deep overpowering sense of loss. Her breathing changed as her chest began to tighten. She tried to look up at him, but he didn't have a face. She gasped and dropped his hand, and then he was gone.

.   .   .

MORNING FINALLY CAME and with it a pretty, heavy-set nurse with a white starched cap and gown, who bustled into the room and drew back the weighty linen curtains. Lillie envied the sprightliness of her step and her healthy, pink cheeks.

"Your friend is gone then, is he?" the nurse said absently as she fluffed the pillows and folded the extra blankets at the end of the bed. "Such a polite fellow, and worried! Gosh, was he worried. He questioned the head nurse as though it were a court of law and he the barrister! Serves her right though. Absolutely a miserable old cow, don't know how any of us work for her." She stopped fussing with the bed and straightened her cap and apron. "Aren't many girls who get to have their hands held all night by a man who looks as he does. Aren't you the lucky one."

Lillie was stunned. What *was* she talking about? It was a moment before she could find any words. "I don't think there was anyone here last night—are you sure it was this room?" She vaguely remembered Primrose and Harry bursting into her room, attempting to stay by her side. Harry had been saying something about getting a guard to stand at her door—it was all a blur—but she did clearly recall the doctor sending them away until the morning.

"Course I am. Lillie Mead, the writer. Attacked in the park yesterday. That's you, ain't it? A wonder they even let him in to see you, much less stay all night. He showed the guard some sort of identification and they didn't give him another glance. Apparently whoever he is is more important than they are! Anyway, that guard is gone now and you have a new one— enormous brute of a man 'e is. Wait till you see 'im!"

"Ah." Her thoughts immediately went back to Harry. Of course it was Harry. How unlike him to spend all night by a hospital bed, but she was touched all the same. He must have pulled out his metaphorical 'Lord' card and played it with relish.

Although what type of identification did he actually show them? She imagined him bossing the doctors and nurses around in his magisterial tone, indignant at the suggestion he leave until morning. "Yes, blond-haired fellow, nice clothes?" She smiled to think of him trying to sleep uncomfortably on a hospital chair.

"No, no, the dark-haired man. Well dressed, I will give you, but not a fair hair on his head. Dashingly tall, rather like Heathcliff might have been. Do you read much Bronte, being American and all?" The nurse stood at the end of the bed with extra grey woollen blankets slung over her arm and waited expectantly for a reply.

Lillie was speechless. She didn't understand what was going on at all.

She sat back in her bed. Something else was niggling at her. It came and went; she tried not to focus on it too intently, in the hopes that something in her subconscious would jog the memory. Although she hadn't see her attacker's face, he had been familiar in some way, although not in a way she could put into words. She remembered the ground coming up to meet her as she fell after being struck, the smell and texture of clothing, pieces muddled together in her fuzzy memory, the taste of mud on her lips. What was it? It was driving her mad. Something, *something* about him she knew. Or perhaps it was just her mind playing tricks on her.

At that moment the door to her room opened and a breathless Primrose came rushing through it, trailing Harry, her sister, and Floyd behind her.

"Lillie! You are awake, I am so pleased. Good morning..." she said towards the nurse, who had decided at that moment to begin rearranging the supplies in the hutch by the bed. "I have been so worried about you! They wouldn't let us stay last night. What an absolutely vile thing for someone to do!" She paused and waited for the nurse to make her way from the room before she continued in a whisper. "Obviously you are onto something and someone doesn't like it."

Lillie's head was beginning to hurt again. She wanted to tell Primrose about last night but decided, given that she felt horrendous and had little energy, that making a fuss about something she didn't understand would only worry everyone unnecessarily.

"Thank God you are all right," Floyd said, stepping forward and clasping her hand. "Your sister and I have been so worried about you."

The look on Penny's face was anguished. "Please, say you will come back to New York with us, this is...it's insane for you to be doing this job," she said, begging.

Lillie's mouth felt dry and she was beginning to feel very warm. She pushed the covers away from her body.

Her sister continued. "What happened? I told you to wait for a taxi! Frightful day it was with all that rain. Honestly, and they say New York is dangerous." Penny fiddled with the bed linens, folding and straightening them, then running her hands over them, again and again, attempting to smooth them.

"Did you happen to see your attacker?" Floyd asked gravely.

Lillie shook her head. She had very little recollection of what had occurred in the park. She didn't remember a thing past the man's boots hitting her squarely in the jaw and a wrinkled coat. She shuddered, and felt Harry's eyes on her.

"Right!" he interjected. "I shall go and collect Rumple from the station and then Penny and I will file a police report on this incident—Penny was the last one to see you before you were attacked and I want to ensure myself this is dealt with swiftly. Lillie, my friend, please just rest."

"Not bloody likely. I am coming with you," Lillie said, attempting to get up.

"As am I," Floyd added.

"Oh no, you aren't," Harry said, sternly pushing her back

down onto the bed. "You will be here overnight, and tomorrow we will re-evaluate with your doctor. You have had a serious blow to the head and they need you in for observation." He turned to Floyd. "Thank you for the offer of accompaniment, but I think three of us will just overwhelm them. If its all the same to you, I think it should just be one family member in there—the last thing we want is to get Scotland Yard's back up."

Lillie frowned at him. "Would you kindly open that window? I need some cool air."

Penny started towards it but Floyd jumped up. "Please, allow me." As Floyd struggled with the rusted latch, the other three gathered up their coats. The latch of the window finally gave way and she felt the blissful rush of cool air into the room.

Harry said, "Oh, incidentally, with all this happening, I forgot to tell you. We found the man who bribed Worley."

"What a stroke of luck! Where is he now?" Lillie was excited, but dizzy, and all their faces were looking unnatural to her. Colours swirled around their heads while the backdrop of the room became a jagged haze.

"In the morgue, I'm afraid. Pushed off a bridge, apparently. But we are hopeful that whoever killed him is also Lady Swindon's killer—and likely your attacker, come to think of it. It makes sense," Harry said, looking grim. "Constable Worley saw the story about his death and came to London to offer his assistance."

"And all of this has happened while I sit here in this stuffy hospital. I need to get out of here immediately."

"Soon enough. I will be back in the morning to collect you. In the meantime, stop blustering and get some rest," Harry told her. He opened the door and ushered everyone out.

An enormous figure in the hallway stood aside to let them pass.

Harry turned back and gave her a wink. "Your bodyguard—ex-soldier, Special Forces."

"Seems very extravagant," Lillie said.

"Better safe than sorry."

Lillie nodded. Perhaps they had been far too cavalier to this point. It was becoming painfully obvious that Lady Swindon's murderer would do whatever it took to thwart their efforts, even if it meant trying to kill her. None of them were safe.

Her head throbbed. Obviously whatever medication they were giving her was making her drowsy. Giving them a little wave from her bed, she drifted off to sleep again, this time with ease.

20

HARRY

HARRY WATCHED WITH amusement as Rumple attempted to manhandle three large cases off of the third-class car and onto the station floor. His normal pristine affect was marred by the glistening of sweat from his efforts. *Classic Rumple*, Harry thought, *bringing far more clothing than any one man would ever need – and him a servant no less.* He had half a mind to help him, but didn't want to ruin the entertainment. Throngs of passengers pushed past Rumple as he straightened up to scan the crowd. Harry gave him a wave and made his way over.

"I must say, I am relieved to see you, old sport. Thank you for coming. Are all these cases yours? Never one to travel light, are you?" Harry attempted to lift one of the cases, but buckled under its enormous weight. "What on earth have you got in here? It weighs a bloody ton!"

"Firearms, sir, and some other essentials, but nothing to bother you with."

"You really do take protection seriously, Rumple—I didn't realize we even had any firearms."

"Did you think those boot-room cupboards were full of boots?" he scoffed. "Hardly, sir."

"You *are* a dark horse. Trade me for a lighter case, would you?" They exchanged suitcases, and the two of them made their way away from the platform to the hired car outside the station.

As they walked through the crowd, Harry thought with irritation back to the phone call he had with the newspaper that morning. Jeremy Winston could be the most infuriating man. Harry had relayed the recent course of events to him and suggested Lillie should return to Oxford immediately upon her release from the hospital. It was no longer safe for her to continue in London, and Winston could re-task her to another, safer section—community events, perhaps, or parish news. Harry had every intention of putting her and Primrose on a train by tomorrow afternoon and carrying on alone. Winston hadn't immediately agreed, instead asking to speak with Lillie. Harry knew that would result in Lillie stubbornly refusing to be taken off the case—which was precisely his reason for calling Winston while Lillie was absent. Silly fool. Well never mind, he didn't need Winston's blessing on how to proceed.

Spotting his hired car near the curb, the men pushed their way through the revolving doors, awkwardly banging the trunks as they did so. Harry cursed under his breath at Rumple's extravagant packing. One would have thought they were traveling with the Prince of Wales.

"Just here." Harry motioned with his chin, unable to free his hands.

They began to load the cases into the boot of the car. Glancing at his watch, Harry realized he was going to be late to meet Penny if they didn't get moving. "Honestly, Rumple, could you not have secured your weapons here in the city rather than lugging them all the way from Oxford? What on earth is in there anyway, cannons? It isn't war time, you know."

"It is for me, sir. If someone thinks they can attack Miss Mead and get away with it, they had better think again. A friend of the Green family is a friend of mine. And let us leave no precious man behind to face the guns or treachery, alone."

"Well, that's the spirit anyway," Harry said, slapping him on the back as they got in the car. He spoke to the driver. "Claridge's, and quickly please. Picking up one and then carrying on to Victoria Embankment."

NEW SCOTLAND YARD was teeming with overworked detectives and efficient clerical secretaries dressed in the same muted drab colours of the interior walls. The air was filled with the hum of typewriters and hushed conversation, punctuated by the occasional ring of the telephone.

"And I thought *I* had an uphill battle with my drawing room walls—this is an abomination," Harry whispered loudly as he and Penny made their way to the front desk. "Do you remember a few years back when you and Lillie first came to the Winter Ball at that ghastly house—the MacKinnons, was it? We had only just met, and you and I had the most delightful time trying to pinpoint the source of that horrendous smell in the dining room." Penny nodded distractedly. He knew she wasn't really listening, but he was desperately trying to keep their moods light. "Well," Harry continued, "I believe I smell something similar now..."

They arrived at the desk and Harry cleared his throat. A middle-aged officer looked up from his desk, peering at them over his iron-rimmed reading glasses, obviously annoyed at the intrusion.

"Yes?" he said impatiently.

"My name is Harry Green and I have come to report an assault that occurred yesterday in the park."

"Yesterday? Well, we obviously have a stone-cold trail to follow now—why wasn't this reported earlier? Are you the victim?"

"I suppose it should have been reported earlier, however, when I telephoned in the incident last night I was told in no uncertain terms that there was no one on duty at that time who could take my statement. Apparently, all your officers were otherwise occupied at a quarrel somewhere else in the city. And, to answer your question, no, I am not the victim. I am reporting on behalf of a young woman who, as a result of the incident, is in hospital. This is her sister," Harry said, nodding toward Penny, "and I am her friend."

"Hmph." The officer took a pad of legal paper from a desk drawer and began a reluctant inquiry. "Name of victim?"

"Lillie Mead."

"Age of victim?"

"28 years."

"Injuries as a result of the attack?"

"Head injuries, lacerations to the face and neck, bruising..."

The officer cut him off.

"Did the victim see her attacker?"

"Not really, only to say he was male and wearing some sort of an oilskin coat and boots."

"Short, tall?"

"I am not sure. Tall enough to bludgeon her over the head."

"Was she...interfered with?"

Penny gasped.

"No, thank God."

"Have a seat. I'll have you report to an officer to make an official statement. It won't be long."

The two of them sat down on the worn and cracked leather seats provided in the waiting area, while Rumple chose to stand at attention. Harry detected the faint smell of years of body odour emanating from his chair.

"Well," he said, with false brightness for Penny's sake. "We shall catch this scoundrel and see what he has to say for himself." His words sounded hollow even to his ears.

Penny's face was strained and exhausted. "Harry, I want to take Lillie home with me once she is well enough to travel. I don't blame anyone for what has happened here, but I think she should return to New York. She doesn't belong here."

Harry said nothing in reply.

He waited a minute, then changed the subject. "I don't suppose there is anywhere to get a cup of tea in here while we wait?" He looked to Rumple, who mutely shook his head. "Shame..." Harry gingerly brushed off the arms of the chair he was sitting in, wondering why they didn't keep better care of the waiting room. It was filthy.

The better part of an hour passed before a sharp-featured, middle-aged detective with intelligent green eyes showed them into his office.

"Have a seat," he commanded as they crowded into the small, cramped room. The detective's desk was covered in piles of papers, and he made no effort to clear them. He peered at them over one particularly large stack of files, then leaned forward and retrieved a pen from the far side of his desk. "I understand you are reporting an attack in the park from yesterday. Any idea why she may have been attacked?"

Harry hadn't really thought through what he would say.

The detective wasn't the patient type. "Let me put it to you another way. Is there anyone who would wish her harm?"

"Of course not!" Penny exclaimed.

"Well...that isn't exactly true..." *Here goes*, thought Harry. "Lillie is a reporter for the Oxford Daily Press and she is currently writing a column on the murder of a Lady Eleanor Swindon from a few months ago. The Oxford police did little to investigate, because one of the leading investigators on the case was the subject of bribery. The source of the bribe was killed last night in London. His name was Hewitt Darcy."

The detective didn't look as though he was having any trouble keeping up with Harry's story. "You think this Darcy fellow was the man who attacked Miss Mead?"

"No, he was already dead by then, but it's likely that whoever attacked Miss Mead also had this man killed."

"Tell me more about the Swindon case."

"It is believed Lady Swindon, of Oxfordshire incidentally, not London, was poisoned. When the police dropped the investigation, Lady Swindon's son, Edgar, came to me and I offered to look into the case for him."

"And you are a private investigator?" Harry couldn't tell if the detective was mocking him or not.

"Certainly not. Edgar is a friend from school and it was obvious the police mismanaged the case, although at the time I hadn't a clue why. The miscarriage of justice bothered me, so I felt it was something that should be noted publicly in the press."

"Interesting. So you are doing the work an incompetent police force chose not to?"

"Precisely," Harry said.

"And where exactly are you at in this investigation?" *Yes,* Harry thought, *he is mocking me.*

"Well, Lady Swindon's husband is a bit of a cold fish, but I suppose poor manners don't necessarily make a killer."

"*Lord* Swindon? A killer?" The detective stifled an incredulous laugh.

"Yes, *Lord* Swindon." Harry was getting annoyed. "Status in life doesn't guarantee an adherence to the law." The detective remained silent. Harry continued, "I think if we can trace the movements of this Darcy fellow before his death, we could probably track down Lady Swindon's killer."

"Possibly, yes."

"Have you got anything on the fellow you might care to share?"

"With a civilian? Of course not. I suggest you take this Miss Mead out of the equation, go back to Oxford, and leave this matter to the police."

"Is that so?" Harry said curtly. "And *I* suggest you read the papers, detective. You never know—you might find a clue as to who killed Lady Swindon, *if* you care to look." He looked towards Penny and nodded. "Let's go."

Harry quickly stood and ushered a protesting Penny to the door. He practically had to drag her down the hall after him.

"Harry! I think you are overreacting," she sputtered behind him. "Harry?" She bumped into the back of him as Harry stopped dead in his tracks. To the left of them was an open office door. Inside were two men deep in conversation who had yet to notice them. Harry glanced in quickly and remained just long enough to be sure he was seeing things correctly. He then took Penny to the waiting area to collect Rumple.

As they emerged onto the street, Harry knew for certain what he had just seen:

Lord Swindon, speaking to a detective and looking quite comfortable as he did it.

21

HARRY

B Y THE TIME HARRY'S HIRED CAR returned to Claridge's, it was well after seven o'clock. He had dropped Penny back at her hotel and then carried on with Rumple, emerging now through the front doors of their hotel exhausted. He noted it was beginning to feel remarkably like home. The checkerboard floor and mahogany front desk were a welcome retreat from the world outside, its cold and wet banished by the warm glow of the fireplace. He had been in London too long.

"Shall we?" Harry said, motioning to the bar, almost tasting the whiskey on his tongue and wondering in passing if wanting a drink more than he ever wanted food was something to be concerned about?

Rumple nodded. *Was he reading his mind or answering his question?*

Primrose had planned to return to the hospital for final visiting hours, so he wasn't expecting her back for—he glanced at his watch, a beautiful rose-gold Vacheron with a suspect ability to keep proper time—at least another hour. His stomach growled cavernously. He hadn't eaten since his rushed breakfast that morning, and there hadn't been time during the day what with running between the hospital, train station, and Scotland Yard. He would satiate it now with a warm, peaty amber and feed it later.

The bar area was full, so Harry commandeered a table for two in a far dark corner of the room, away from the swinging kitchen doors, in the hopes they could talk freely without being overheard. He wanted to get Rumple's opinion on their afternoon. They settled in and the bartender nodded at them that Harry's usual was on the way—*he really had been in London too long*.

"Swindon at the Yard. What is your take on that?"

"Obviously he is working with them on something. Either this or—"

"Well, what else would it be? Of course it's about his wife's murder!" Harry hadn't meant to interrupt, but couldn't help himself.

Rumple's eyes were watching something behind Harry's chair. Harry opened his mouth to give him hell for his lack of attention, but Rumple gave an almost imperceptible shake of his head, silencing him.

"Hello," a voice came from behind him. Irish. Soft. Hesitant.

Harry turned to see Blackie, wringing his hat in his hands. *Had he been listening to them?*

"Oh, hello," Harry said, startled. A moment of awkward silence ensued, before he remembered his manners. "Please sit...have a drink." Harry nodded to Rumple, who retrieved a chair from a neighbouring table and signalled to the bartender to bring another whiskey.

"Am I interrupting?" Blackie looked unsure of himself as he tentatively sat down.

"Not at all. Rumple, meet Blackie. Blackie, this is my...my friend. Rumple." The two men nodded warily at each other. Rumple got up and, without a word, left the table.

"He likes to give me my privacy," Harry said, feeling the need to explain. Rumple didn't tend to observe social niceties.

Blackie nodded.

"What brings you back here?"

"I didn't finish telling you why I came to London to find Ms. Mead. Is she around?" he asked, scanning the room.

Harry didn't want to discuss Lillie's attack. He decided it was better to keep mum on the subject—especially with someone he knew little about.

"Not tonight—you just have me here, I am afraid." Was that disappointment on his face? "I assure you, whatever you tell me I will relay to Lillie—we are interchangeable."

Blackie nodded, apparently satisfied. He rubbed the back of his neck anxiously for a few moments. "Actually...." he began, looking around the room, "oh, never mind, I don't know why I came. I'm sorry to disturb." Before Harry could say anything the man was up and pushing back his chair.

"Now, stop right there!" Harry barked. "If you think I am going to let you march out of here without telling me for the second time this week what you are doing here in London, then you better think again."

Rumple, watching from the bar, raised his eyebrows at Harry's tone and began to make his way back to the table. Harry held up his hand, pre-empting the interruption. He wanted the Irishman to himself.

"Just what the hell are you doing here and how are you involved in all this?" Harry leaned forward in as menacing a stance as he could manage while sitting down, noting the surprise on Blackie's face at his tone.

The Irishman carefully sat back down and there was an uncomfortable pause before he spoke. When he finally did, it came in a rush of words that seemed as though they had been pent up for years. "I am a father. Edgar is my son." Even he looked startled by his own abrupt admission.

Harry thought about this for a moment. "I did wonder. The chap looks nothing like his father—Lord Swindon, I mean."

"We were found out. The head groom knew of our affair and he knew the child was mine. He threatened Ellie and blackmailed her for *thirty years*. And she paid it, and refused to see me again, until..."

"Until recently, when she visited you in Ireland."

Blackie nodded, his eyes downcast.

Why was he telling him all this? To point the finger of blame at Lord Swindon? To say he was the scorned, murderous husband?

"She came to tell me she wasn't going to be coerced by him anymore. That she was going to tell her husband about Edgar, that he was mine, that she was getting too old to lie anymore and she didn't care about consequences. She knew I had never married, through a cousin of hers, she told me that she...that she...still loved me. Oh—" he gasped, apparently too emotional to finish.

Harry believed the angst was real but wondered if his explanation, and the timing of it, wasn't just a little too convenient.

"Where were you last night?" he asked, knowing it sounded terribly rude after Blackie's confession, but Lillie was lying in a hospital bed and he was angry.

"Last night? Why?"

Was the confusion on his face a ruse? He hadn't answered Harry's question. Was he buying time to come up with an alibi?

"Because I asked you." Harry kept his voice deliberately benign.

"Uh...at the room I am renting in Pimlico, I guess. I had a light dinner down the street at a pub and then returned home around nine. I don't understand. Why are you asking me this? Has something happened?"

Was the concern genuine? Harry didn't know. If he was lying, he was damn good at it.

"Never mind." It was no good, Lillie was a much better interrogator than he was. He gave way to his sympathy about the man's story. "Tell me about Lady Swindon's final visit to Ireland —tell me about it all."

The candlelight flickered off the Irishman's face, hollowing out the dark circles beneath his ebony eyes as he began to speak. Harry listened on as a clock chimed behind the bar and cigarette smoke swirled above their heads while he watched the doorway, expectant for Primrose to arrive, every other person entering through it a disappointment. All the while, lilting Irish-accented words filled his ears, reminding him of how far they had come, and how much farther they would need to go, to find the truth.

22

LILLIE

T HE CLOCK IN THE HALL OF the hospital corridor struck 1 a.m., but its gong was masked by a curious popping sound and the sound of rushing wind.

Lillie was drifting in and out of consciousness, but the smell of something like charred applewood and burnt supper punctuated her relaxed state. She drew up, alert, and with some difficulty crept slowly out of her bed to the closed door. She put her hand on the doorknob and leapt back with a cry at the blazing hot metal. It was then that she noticed smoke was coming from underneath the door. It took her a moment to register what was going on, for her body to be fully awake and her mind to begin working logically.

Then she was flooded with an overwhelming dread. "Fire! Fire!" she cried, beginning to panic.

Where was everyone? Why hadn't the alarms gone off? She had to get out! She would die if she stayed any longer. Frantically, she rushed around the room, searching for another way out. Her chest and eyes burned from the smoke and heat that was rapidly accumulating now in her room.

She ran to the window, but the latch was stuck again and

she remembered, fleetingly, Floyd struggling with it earlier in the day. Why was it closed again, for God's sake? Hadn't she told him to leave it open? Although even if it had been open, it was barred on the outside with a thick metal mesh. Maybe she could have kicked it out. At least there would have been air...blissful, fresh, life-saving air.

No, she decided, there was now only one way out, and that was through the hallway, which was by now likely overrun with flames. She rushed to the wash basin and wet a long strip of fresh bandaging the nurse had left, holding it to her mouth. Then she took another strip of bandaging and used it to open the door. The flames leapt into her room and she instinctively fell to the floor and began crawling into the hallway, pressing the bandaging to her mouth as she used her other hand for balance. The fire devoured the oxygen in her room behind her like an insatiable monster to its prey.

The hall outside was apocalyptic. Door frames and the waiting room furniture were alight with flames, the empty nurse's station now engulfed in the blaze. Shards of glass cut her knees as she dragged herself along the scorching floor, thick black smoke obscuring her vision. Which way should she go? Choosing left, she scuttled along the floor, praying she wouldn't faint before she found the stairwell.

Crawling along as fast as she could, unsure of how much farther the stairwell was, she bumped into something. A solid, unyielding mass—human. Peering through the smoke, she saw it was a bloodied arm and recoiled, realizing it was the body of her enormous guard. His head and arm lay at an unnatural angle, and she fought the urge to vomit. She quickly felt his neck for a pulse, but there was none. She steeled herself and tried dragging him by his feet, but his dead weight only shifted the slightest bit, her body weakened by injury to her ribs not allowing her to have her full strength, and she couldn't stand up to get a better grip or she would certainly be devoured by the flames.

The heat on her face was unbearable. She screamed and screamed for help but the sound of the roaring flames drowned out her voice like a torrent of rushing water. Still she tried to drag the man, only managing to move a few feet down the hallway. She would perish if she stayed here any longer, but she couldn't bear to leave him.

All at once she was grabbed from behind and pulled away from the guard. Sputtering, she cried out and fought against the arms that wrapped around her as she was pulled along the corridor at surprising speed. She was losing the strength in her legs, her head dizzy from the smoke. Her feet dragged, and she felt her body sagging.

The unknown person continued to pull her; she felt the cool rush of air as they reached the end of the hallway. Down the stairs she went, her feet hitting each step as they made their way to the main floor. At the landing, her abductor threw her over his shoulders as he continued down the second set of stairs. She could feel the fabric of the man's overcoat brushing painfully across her heated face as he ran. The smell of burning hair filled her nostrils, and she realized it was her own. She tried to speak.

"The guard..." she rasped.

"He is dead," a voice came back.

They reached the front doors of the hospital just as the fire brigade pushed through the lobby, dragging great lengths of hose in from the street. The night air felt cool on her face and she was grateful for the drizzling rain.

"Please," she croaked. "I can walk."

But the man ignored her and kept going down the sidewalk, his grip on the back of her legs like iron. She struggled against him, but he didn't slow his pace. He was terribly strong and Lillie began to panic.

"Stop, stop!" she cried as the man again broke into a run. She couldn't believe he could run with her body slung over him. She felt like a sack of potatoes, but the more she struggled, the firmer he held.

When they reached the end of the second block the man darted to the left into a large, fenced garden that appeared to belong to a row of beautiful new Edwardian town homes, their ivory facades lit only by the occasional flicker of a cloud-veiled moon. He made his way into the darkest middle, under the canopy of an enormous bare maple tree. There he stopped and slowly released her onto the leaf-soaked earth, leaning her gently against the great trunk of the tree.

Her nightgown glowed white against the darkened night and she looked up at the crouched man's face. He had miraculously not lost his hat in the escape from the fire, and he now pulled the collar of his coat up higher around the bottom of his face. She peered at him, trying to make out his features.

"Why...did you take me here..." she gasped, coughing. She tried to clear her throat but the smoke felt etched onto it.

He didn't say anything. She began to shake, with fear or cold, she wasn't sure. The man removed his coat, very carefully pulling his scarf around his face as he gently leaned forward to wrap the coat around her shoulders.

Through the smell of the smoke and her singed hair she caught a hauntingly familiar scent from the coat. Cedar and rose. Her mind reeled. She reached up and snatched the scarf from his face, and let out a cry.

It was Jack.

23

LILLIE

T HE SCARF WAS SOFT IN HER hands, and she clutched at it as though it were a life line.

"Oh! It's you! Oh God, no...no it can't be."

Her voice sounded hysterical in her ears. She must be delirious with the smoke—it couldn't be him. She tried to get to her feet, but her legs were weak. She couldn't get up, but she couldn't stay there either.

She needed to think. Quickly.

He was dead, wasn't he? Of course he was.

They had told her that. *Officials* had told her that. Why would they lie?

She had mourned him for two years. Two years of darkness, two years of drowning, two years of emptiness. And yet here, on this horrible night, here this...this...*imposter* stood. Right in front of her. Torturing her.

The man who could not possibly be Jack stayed crouched beside her, his eyes afraid. He reached out to touch her and she recoiled. He let his hand fall. Lillie frantically rubbed her eyes with her soot-covered hands, clouding her vision.

"Tell me you aren't who I think you are—this must be a

dream, a horrible trick." She began to cry, great uncontrollable sobs escaping her throat, her head swimming with memories.

The man watched her for a few seconds and then swiftly pulled her towards him and folded her into his chest, his arms wrapped around her shivering body. He sat there with her, cradling her body like a child and rocking her as she wept.

When he finally spoke, his voice was gentle and instantly recognizable. *How could she have missed it before?* "Yes, it's me. I have so much to tell you, and so much to apologize for. All of it must wait for now. But know this—I love you. I always have and I always will."

Tears rolled down Lillie's face but she couldn't feel them. She couldn't feel the rain anymore either. She was numb with disbelief, amazed that this man, who she thought had perished, was here. But she didn't understand. Why hadn't he reached out to her? Had he only just found his way back to England? Was he a prisoner of war? Where had he *been* for two years? There were too many questions...

She inhaled deeply, wanting the warmth and scent of him to last forever. She wanted it imprinted on her mind, because she didn't really believe it. All the pain of the last few years released from her body like a pent-up storm breaking over the moors and lashing across the fields.

Jack held her as it washed over her, but said finally, objectively, "You are in the gravest danger. Do you understand?"

Lillie fell silent. Suddenly, she pulled away from him and slapped him hard across his face, surprising both of them. Jack said nothing, watching her. She searched his handsome face, watching his cheek redden in the little light from a distant streetlamp. His dark hair was wet now from the rain and it dripped down his neck onto the collar of his shirt. Light blue, each drop darkening it—each passing minute a realization she had been duped, lied to, deceived. He looked slightly older but not much. His face was more carved and tired than it had been, his dark eyes sad.

He was watching the street, glancing this way and that, seemingly uncomfortable with their surroundings. "There will be time for this later, but right now I have to get you away from all of this. Someone has tried to kill you twice and they have only narrowly failed at doing so. I don't plan to give them another chance. Can you walk?" He looked down at her feet. "You have no shoes," he said, stating the obvious. "We need to get to my flat but it is a little ways from here. Here, this should work."

Jack removed a pocket knife from his trousers and made a small slit in his scarf, tearing it into two. He gently took Lillie's sodden feet and wrapped them in the fabric, attempting to fasten the ends together to keep them in place while she walked.

"Whoever started that fire will be looking for you once they realize you've escaped it. We need to stay in the shadows."

Lillie got to her feet, clutching the overcoat to keep warm. She was still angry, but her chilled body and the gravity of the situation she was in wasn't lost on her. They needed to get moving.

"Put it on properly. You need it. You are still shivering." He looked as though he would give her the clothes off his body if she would allow it.

She pulled on the coat and he reached around her shoulders to help her. His touch felt electric on her skin.

"Let's go," he commanded.

They made their way back to the edge of the street, purposefully staying out of the light of the street lamps, the night their ally. Jack led the way and Lillie followed closely behind as they made their way through residential neighbourhoods, past closed coffee shops, butchers and cobblers.

When they had to pass through any area that was lit, Jack

would grab her hand and break into a run. Lillie tried to be unmoved by the feel of his hand in hers, the touch of his skin. It was just as she remembered.

The rain had intensified and they were both soaked through. Adrenaline kept her going, whether from the fear of being killed or the revelation that Jack was alive, she didn't know. Finally, after twenty minutes of painstaking going they reached a small, stone apartment building. Rather than going in the front door, Jack went around back and unlocked the rear door. They made their way up the stairs to the second floor.

Jack's flat was large and tastefully furnished. The high ceilings were rare in the few London apartments Lillie had seen. Jack made his way over to the arched windows facing the street and closed the curtains while he switched on the lighting throughout the room. With the exception of an oak, roll-top desk covered in papers and files, the room was extraordinarily tidy for a man who lived alone. Lillie wondered for a brief moment if perhaps Jack had a girlfriend, or even a wife. They had certainly been apart long enough for that to be a reality.

She stood at the doorway dripping water onto the wooden floor and began to remove the now-sodden overcoat and her makeshift shoes. Jack took them from her and put everything in a wet heap on the kitchen counter.

"There is a bathroom just there." He pointed to the right of the living room. "Get in a warm bath immediately. In the meantime I will make some tea and find you something to wear."

Lillie nodded wearily.

As she ran the bath she removed her hospital nightgown and looked in the mirror. The hair on the left side of her face was singed and now reached just below her chin, giving her face a lopsided look, which admittedly made her look ridiculous. She searched for some scissors in the vanity and was oddly relieved to find nothing that alluded to a woman living there. The whole situation of him being alive, and her looking for evidence of a wife or girlfriend, while she snooped through his personal belongings was ludicrous. She set to work on her hair, cutting off the right side so it matched the left. When she was finished, her long locks filled the sink, but she felt she hadn't done a bad job. These bobs were all the rage now anyway, so at least she had joined the modern century.

She got into the bath and felt the warm water envelope her skin. She couldn't believe where she was and everything that had happened to her in one evening. The attack, the fire, the escape, the dead guard outside her door, and finding the only man she had ever really loved alive and well and living in London. Her head was swimming.

She washed her skin with Jack's soap. Cedar and rose...of course. A sharp stab of nostalgia knifed through her. She had tried to find that same soap in New York after he had died so she could smell him again and hold onto his memory. She had searched every perfumery, pharmacy and department store in the city, only to come up empty handed. And yet here it was, in a small white bathroom, in a flat in London, on a street she didn't know. *Here* it had been all along.

She towelled off and wondered what she should do now that she had no clothes. A tap on the door interrupted her thoughts. She wrapped the towel around herself and opened it. Jack had changed and he now stood before her in a soft grey sweater and dark pyjama bottoms. He was holding some clothes in his hand, but instead of handing them to her, he stood very still. He looked at her intently, his eyes never moving from her face.

"You cut your hair," he said eventually.

"I had to. It was mostly gone anyway."

"It looks beautiful." He handed her the clothing and she closed the door.

A few minutes later she emerged, dressed in a rolled-up

pair of men's pyjamas. They were enormous on her, but thankfully the waist had a drawstring to keep them up.

"Please come sit down. I have some tea and I made some sandwiches. You must be ravenous. You need food and sleep," he said, then caught sight of himself in a living room mirror. He touched his face, smudging black freckles of soot into a long, fingered line. "I apparently *also* need a bath." He risked a little smile.

"What time is it?" Lillie didn't smile back.

"Around 3 a.m. Please sit." She did as she was told and he poured her a cup of tea and put some food on a plate. He sat down across from her on a navy-blue Queen Anne chair and watched her. Lillie nibbled on the sandwiches, realizing she was indeed very hungry. She tried not to be conscious of Jack's gaze.

"Feel better?" he asked.

When she didn't answer him, he continued in a different vein.

"We need a plan now, for you. You are in terrible danger."

"I am going to need to write my column—immediately. I should get back to Claridge's as soon as possible. Harry and Primrose will be worried."

"That is certainly *not* the plan I had in mind."

"Well, I can't very well stay here."

"Of course you can. I can do some investigating in the morning—I have no doubt that fire wasn't started by accident. At least then I can get closer to who is doing all this. Give me a day."

Lillie sighed and put her plate down. She looked directly into his dark eyes, angry at herself for feeling a flutter in her stomach as she did so. "I don't think you really understand the situation. Until tonight I thought you were dead. You let me believe for two years that you were dead. When I heard you were gone I went into the most enormous black hole—I never thought I would emerge from it. My life changed. I went back to New York and I tried to go on, eventually. But I didn't really become a whole person again until Harry wrote to me and I came to work on the mystery of Lady Swindon's death. I got a job at the newspaper. I began writing again. All of sudden I could breathe normally and envision a life for myself—a life without you. Then, out of nowhere, you re-emerge."

Jack remained silent.

She went on. "You dragged me out of a fire—how did you even know I was there? Were you following me?"

"I had to. I won't apologize. I am glad I did."

"How long have you been following me?" A sudden realization occurred to her. "Were you in New York? I saw a man outside my window after one of Penny's parties one night."

"Yes. I was there on an assignment and I wanted to see you."

She was surprised by his directness and wondered what assignment he was talking about.

"And here in London, in the park that day?"

"I couldn't get to you in time. I saw you leave your sister's hotel and you must have taken a turn I didn't anticipate—when I found you, someone else had gotten there first. I am so sorry. Thankfully I scared him off before he killed you and managed to get you to the hospital."

"That *was* you!"

Jack nodded.

"I don't understand!" she cried, frustrated and on the verge of tears. "Why did you wait so long? Why did you do this to me?"

"I made a mistake," he said fiercely. "I thought you were in love with someone else. And it was better, for so many reasons, for me to leave you as you were—happy with another. There is too much to explain...it's so very complicated." He shook his head.

"Who?" Lillie sputtered, confused.

"Andrew. That American soldier, I saw you with him...at that fundraiser in Mayfair, I thought it was him anyway...I had never met him before, of course, but I knew you were once in love with him. And there you were—dancing with him—and I just assumed..."

"Assumed what?" She wanted answers. Immediate answers. And she wanted to hear him say everything out loud so there wasn't any confusion.

"Well, that after I left for the war that you had forgotten me and decided to take him back and get married after all. I was cut up about it and I didn't stay to ask questions. Afterwards I was approached by special branch, a division of the SIS, and offered a job. I took it. At the time I had nothing to lose, or so I thought. I thought you were gone from me forever. I felt dead inside."

"What on earth are you talking about? So you faked your own death? You became a *spy*," she said, hissing the words at him, "because you thought I was dancing with a man who was my ex-fiancé? Never mind that you didn't get the correct identification on the soldier and completely misread the entire situation! I remember that night very well, and the man I was dancing with was my brother-in-law. How could you be so... so... stupid and so cruel?" She was stuttering, now. Disbelief and anger had given way to confusion and cold and not giving a damn. She was adrift. Unhinged. A new sensation for her.

"I made a mistake. As I said, I saw you dancing with a man whom I thought was your old fiancé. How was I to know it was your brother-in-law? The way you were looking at him, as though you were so comfortable with him—I misread everything. Anyway, the rest is as I have said. I joined a government-sanctioned group responsible for counter-espionage and I let you think I was gone forever. I thought it would be easier that way—for you—that it would allow you the freedom to not feel guilty about marrying Andrew."

"You must know Andrew was a womanizing bastard I was happy to be rid of."

A look of embarrassment crossed Jack's face. "I did know that, but I was never sure you did."

"I am not an idiot and I would hardly accept the company of a man who preferred other women. I would rather be alone. What about your parents? And Harry? Did they know?"

"My parents were in India at the time, but they knew. And Harry...well, he had to get the same story as you. It was safer for me to leave Oxford behind—or so I thought."

"Why was it safer? What did you do? Weren't you in France with your regiment? I have your letters...from France..."

There were so many questions. They flew off her tongue in staccato, punctuating the air around them. His eyes were sad and weary. Behind them lay something she couldn't quite place—so many of the men who saw action during the war had the same haunted look in theirs. As though the ghosts of war were forever with them, following them through their lives. As though they were living with death every waking moment.

"All I can say in explanation is this: the Germans were killing our soldiers, hundreds upon hundreds of them, daily. The fields smelled of death, of rotting corpses, of blood and earth, of sickness and damp..." he said, shivering. "Even *our own* officers were cavalier with our lives. We hardly needed the Germans to kill us—we were doing that job ourselves just fine. We needed something, anything, to change. And I had a chance to do more than be cannon fodder—to get into the German psyche, to get into their heads, to change the course of war. It was important work..."

Here he paused, as though he wanted to say more. Instead, he folded his napkin neatly and put it on the table. She waited, but he said no more.

Overpowered by her emotions, she also remained quiet and

an uncomfortable silence filled the space. They sat across from each other but were worlds apart.

Finally she spoke. "But don't you see? *We* died in the process."

Jack nodded, his eyes welling up. "I see that now. Is there any way we could—"

Lillie interrupted him. "I am tired. All of a sudden I feel so very tired."

Jack stood up. "Come with me."

He led her down the hallway and into what was clearly his bedroom. She stopped in her tracks at a picture of herself on the bedside table, remembering when it was taken. They had been at Harry's annual summer party and there had been a hired photographer who snapped their picture as they had sipped raspberry lemonade on the yellowing grass in front of the house. They were smiling at the camera and their faces had a youth and innocence that four years of war had erased from not only them, but from an entire generation. A heavy sadness came over her. She missed those two people in the picture, their hands clasped and eyes bright as though the world was a good and kind place.

She looked at him, but he said nothing. She climbed into the perfectly made bed and he pulled the covers over her. Within a few minutes she was asleep.

WHEN SHE WOKE, daylight was peeking through the closed curtains in the bedroom. The smell of coffee and bacon wafted from the kitchen and she could hear the faint clink of dishes. She padded into the living room and quietly watched as Jack darted between setting two places at a small, round table and the stove to flip whatever he had in the frying pan. She waited and watched him for a few minutes, unobserved. He wore a soft, pinstriped, cotton dress shirt and a pair of dark, charcoal trousers. His hair was wet from the bath and Lillie was at once overcome by the fact by that he was here. Here and in this room and very much alive.

With his back to her, he said, "Good morning, did you sleep well?"

She was startled. She hadn't thought he noticed her.

"I didn't think you knew I was here." She let out a small laugh.

"I am pretty good at reading my surroundings without actually looking."

"Must be an occupational benefit."

"It is. Come and have some breakfast."

She made her way to the table and sat down while he poured her coffee and set some cream and sugar in front of her.

"Do you still take your coffee the same way, extra cream and easy on the sugar?"

Lillie nodded, surprised he remembered. Jack put their breakfast plates on the table and took his seat across from her.

"Let's get down to business, shall we?" he said.

She took a sip of her coffee and waited expectantly.

"I will go back to the hospital this morning and see what I can find out about who started the fire. You will stay here. Under no circumstances will you leave."

"Don't be ridiculous. As I said last night, I have to get back to Harry and Primrose. They will be worried about where I am."

"I have already taken care of it. I sent a man to fetch them this morning and bring them here. I am absolutely certain Harry is being tailed. The man I sent works for me and he is very good at losing tails," Jack said. "None of you can go back to Claridge's. All four of us will use this flat as our base until you can return to Oxford."

"I have to write my column. And where will we all sleep?"

"If you still insist on writing that column, you may use my desk and typewriter and I will get your work to the newspaper. I have a spare bedroom where Harry and I can sleep and you and Primrose can share my bedroom. Since I am the only one of us they aren't aware of, I will do our running around."

"But my sister?"

"I can send word to her hotel that you are safe and secure, but I am not going to bring anyone else here to our base. Not even your sister. The more people that know where we are, the harder it will be to keep it secure. Are we clear?"

Lillie nodded a reluctant agreement, surprised and a little resentful at Jack's take-charge attitude. Who did he think he was, barging in and attempting to take charge of their investigation? They ate their breakfast in silence, his eyes on her the whole time.

Jack stood and went to the hall closet to retrieve his coat. "I will be back before noon. Do not leave this flat under any circumstances, do you understand?"

He walked back over to the kitchen and stood before her chair, close enough for her to smell that soap again. Very slowly he reached down and touched her hair, winding a strand gently around his finger. She sat absolutely still, letting him really touch her for the first time. Then he put his finger ever so softly under her chin, leaning over and drawing his face down to hers. She moved her body back and away from him and the moment was gone. He straightened up and she saw a flicker of hurt in his eyes.

He nodded and was gone.

24

THE ODOUR FROM THE ROYAL London Hospital's second floor charred remains could be smelled down the street. The rain from the previous night had stopped and the sun was peeking through the clouds, attempting to breathe optimism on an area of London that was hell bent on ignoring it.

Fire crews were still stationed outside the main doors to the hospital and patients were being evacuated in an orderly lineup, ambulances coming and going from all over the city.

Jack stood for a moment on the sidewalk, assessing the scene before making his way inside the building. He flashed his credentials to a fireman guarding the stairwell to the second floor.

"Lead investigator in there now, sir. Watch your step—he's about as friendly as a grizzly bear." He nodded at Jack and stood aside, letting him pass.

Jack made his way to the central atrium where the nurses' station had once stood. All that remained was a scorched metal filing cabinet and a charred iron base with a tangled mess of copper wiring. Anything that had been made of wood was completely incinerated.

A middle-aged man with razor sharp eyebrows knitted together in a permanent scowl looked up from his clipboard. "Who are you?"

"Jack Abbott, SIS."

"Intelligence Service, hey? What do you want with the likes of a little hospital fire?"

Jack sized up the man. Small in stature, lacking in confidence—making up for it with an abundance of posturing and ego. It was obvious the investigator didn't want any intrusion into his sphere of influence. Jack had his standard response at the ready. "That is classified for the time being."

"Oh, *classified,* is it." The investigator drew out the words and dripped them with sarcasm.

Jack ignored him. "Any idea where the fire was started?"

"Looks like outside that room just there." The investigator pointed in the direction of Lillie's room. "One deceased outside that door, probably from smoke inhalation."

Jack knew from seeing the dead guard last night that he most certainly hadn't died from the smoke. Lack of oxygen didn't result in a man's neck looking like that. He made his way down the blackened corridor to the area outside the room. The dead guard had been removed, a faint outline of where his body had been remained in the soot.

"Find anything on the man's body? Anything in his clothing? Identification?" Jack called back down the hallway.

"A few coins, keys..." The investigator rummaged around in a couple of metal tins that were labeled and lined up against the wall. His makeshift investigative office. "Oh, and this." He held up something Jack couldn't see from where he was standing. "Poor fellow must have been going out for a smoke, pity he didn't make it. It had to be pried out of his hands—glad I don't have to do that job." He tossed the object to Jack, who caught it handily. It was a cigarette lighter, now charred. While its edges were melted, the engraving on its front was not. It was of a sailboat of some sort.

Jack held it up. "Mind if I take this for analysis? I'll see to it that it is returned to you within forty-eight hours."

"Go ahead. It's been catalogued and photographed."

Jack turned his attention back to the hospital room Lillie had been staying in. It was completely destroyed—a twisted metal bed frame, the mattress long gone, was still smoking. Shards of glass littered the floor. The windows had all, except one, been blown out, the remaining one darkened with an indelible black ash. The mesh outside the windows remained, the paint on it melted away, the metal now charred. Jack shuddered to think what would have happened to Lillie had she not woken in time. Anything organic or made from wood or fiber was long gone.

Jack went back into the corridor and concentrated on the area around where the guard had died. Whoever started the fire could only have done so after he had killed the guard. The door frame to the room had collapsed into the corridor, along with the door. He found a melted door knob and a few blackened hinges.

"Any idea what was used to start the fire?" Jack called back to the inspector.

"You make it sound like it was intentional."

"Well, wasn't it?"

"You can go back and tell your superiors that I don't appreciate your interference in this. But since I can't seem to be able to get rid of you, then yes, I believe it was intentionally started. I haven't got the how or why figured out yet."

"I think I have seen everything I need to see," Jack said, making his way back to the stairwell. "Good day, Inspector."

The inspector looked up from his clipboard with surprise. "That was quick. Care to share anything?"

Jack smiled at him. "You seem to have everything under control. Forgive the intrusion, and good day."

As he made his way down the stairwell Jack turned the item the inspector had let him have in his pocket over and over with this fingers. Metal, engraved, still warm. It was something, anyway.

He hurried. Lillie was at home waiting for him, something he never thought could be a reality. Regardless of the danger that surrounded them, he felt happy for the first time since that picture was snapped, on the yellowing lawn, at Harry's summer garden party such a long time ago. He could still taste the champagne and optimism.

25

HARRY

"HOW DO WE KNOW YOU weren't sent here to kill us?"

The dark car continued at speed through the streets of London taking the most obscure routes, passing by the same landmarks multiple times. Harry was certain this was the third time they had circled Trafalgar Square as he again gazed upward at the statue of Lord Nelson.

The driver didn't look back. "Trust me—if I wanted you dead, we wouldn't be having this conversation right now."

Harry tried not to feel intimidated. He felt for Primrose's hand and gripped it tightly. Lately he had been more daring in his affections and she had responded positively to his advances. Perhaps it was the fear and pace of the mess they were mixed up in, but Harry didn't want to waste any more time dancing around the obvious.

"Are you going to tell me where we are going?" Harry said, leaning forward to get the driver's attention.

"We will be there soon enough."

"I don't understand—you said you knew Lillie's where-abouts, but who sent you?"

"It will all be revealed shortly." The driver was abrupt, interrupting him and effectively ending the conversation.

Harry turned to Primrose. "Not one for idle chit chat, is he? Well, at least we know she is alive. Perhaps I really should have encouraged her more to go back to New York with her sister."

"She wouldn't have gone, no matter what you said. Lillie can make her own decisions," Primrose replied. "Do you think it was wise to leave Rumple at the hotel? Is it safe?"

"Rumple can take care of himself and we need someone there as a go-between. Worley is staying in my room as well, so the two of them can watch for any suspicious activity. I'll check back in with them later this afternoon," Harry said. He attempted a brave smile at Primrose, though brave was something he wasn't quite feeling at the moment. "Are you sure you wouldn't rather be in Oxford working as a governess?" Though he was thrilled she wasn't.

Primrose shook her head as the driver finally pulled up in front of small block of apartments.

"Get ready to jump, sir. Grab the bags as quickly as you can."

Harry did as he was told, handing the smaller cases to Primrose and struggling with the larger ones, thankful she had been more frugal in her packing than Rumple.

"Go around the back of the building and your contact will meet you there. Mind you don't stay out here in the open."

The driver sped off, leaving Harry to wonder again what on earth was going on.

They hurried around the side of building, a tall, black iron fence dividing an impeccably kept gravel walkway from the neighbouring building, and spotted the rear entrance. Harry put the cases down on the crushed gravel and raised his hand to knock on the door, but before he could it was opened abruptly from the inside.

To his utter surprise and dismay, there stood his dead best friend.

"Hello, Harry, old chap." Jack put out his hand as Harry gaped at him and Primrose gasped.

"I...I don't understand..." Harry was stupefied.

"I can explain it all inside. Hello, Primrose, please let me take those from you. Follow me." Jack took their bags and led them up the staircase and into the apartment. Lillie came around a corner to greet them as they walked into the foyer. Harry rushed forward to give her a hug, nearly doing a double take at her new haircut.

"What is happening? There is a ghost in the hallway and you have become a flapper!" he whispered into her ear.

"Well," she said, standing back to look at them all, "it seems that Jack is alive and chose not to tell us until now."

"Lillie, you know I...." Jack started, but Harry interrupted him by walking over and hugging him heartily.

"Welcome back, sport. I thought we were going to have to go through life without you. I'm glad we don't. You obviously have some explaining to do, though."

"Yes, I know. Let's get your things put away and I'll pour us all a drink."

THE FOUR OF them had been talking for hours in the living room when the clock struck seven-thirty and Harry realized his stomach was growling with hunger.

He finally understood the reasoning behind Jack's disappearance, but could see Jack would have an uphill battle if he wanted back in Lillie's good graces. Harry watched her in the candlelight. She seemed distant and removed from the conversation. Her haircut suited her, setting off her high cheekbones and prominent green eyes. The bruises on her face were dissipating, but there was still a dark shade of purple smudged across her chin. She seemed small and vulnerable, clad in men's pyjamas and sitting on her own in an armchair with her legs curled under her.

"You are going to need to get those stitches out," Harry said to her gently. "They don't appear to be holding up very well. Perhaps we could find someone to re-do them for you?"

She nodded and put her hand to her forehead, running her finger across them and twirling a loose piece of thread. Harry noticed Jack watching her, his dark eyes guarded and intense.

"I am famished," Harry said, changing the subject.

"Yes, of course, you must be. I have lots of food. There is some bread and cheese and a stew I bought at the market," Jack said.

"I'll get it ready." Primrose jumped up and Harry joined her in the kitchen, glad of the diversion.

Behind him he heard Jack speak softly to Lillie. "Why don't you let me take those stitches out for you before dinner? Harry is right—they shouldn't be left any longer - I'll see what I can do to fix them so you don't scar too much."

Harry busied himself with setting the table. When he glanced back to the living room, it was empty.

26

LILLIE

L ILLIE SAT ON THE SIDE OF THE bathtub and braced herself for the pain. Pulling up a stool so he was sitting face to face with her, Jack slowly started snipping at her stitches. She could feel her eyes begin to water as he tugged at them, gently trying to remove them. Neither of them spoke as he worked. His face was close to hers and she could smell the whiskey on his breath. She opened her eyes and watched his face as he concentrated on his task. He didn't look at her, his eyes fixed on her stitches. The last few were harder to remove, and he put a hand on her shoulder to steady her as he gave them a sharper tug. She winced and held her breath. And then that part, at least, was over.

Jack took some thread and a needle from a small wooden drawer beside the sink and gathered up a handful of ice from a bowl he had brought in with him. Placing the pieces in a large swath of gauze, he rolled up the fabric and held it to her forehead. She leaned into the pressure, feeling it melt down her cheek, wishing it would numb not only her torn skin, but her insides as well. Perhaps then she could stop thinking about the last few wasted years. When Jack gently began to re-stitch her wound, she felt nothing but the tugging on her flesh and the memory of his abandonment.

Swivelling in his seat to place the needle and thread on the side of the sink next to where he left the scissors, Jack then returned his attention back to her. They sat there like that, he on the stool, she on the side of the tub, as though it was the most natural thing in the world for them to sit, face to face, not speaking, neither of them willing to break the silence.

This time when he leaned in she tilted her chin up and he kissed her so passionately that she nearly fell backwards into the bathtub. He quickly grabbed her, wrapping both arms around her and lifting her up so her body was flat against his, her feet entirely off the ground. He sat her on the side of the sink and pushed his body between her legs as he leaned forward and gently kissed her again. She finally succumbed to him and wrapped her arms around his neck, her fingers entwined in his dark hair, her legs squeezing against his.

But it was only for a moment.

Suddenly she released her hold and pushed him away from her, getting down from the sink and leaving him standing there staring after her.

When she walked into the kitchen Harry and Primrose were already seated at the table. Harry had found a bottle of wine, and upon seeing Lillie's face, quickly poured her a glass. As the deep, red liquid settled in the crystal glass, Harry looked searchingly at her. Ignoring him, she reached for the wine and took a long, thirsty sip, knowing it would take much more than one glass to calm her nerves. She wished Harry had found something stronger.

"I hope you don't mind me not changing for dinner," she joked halfheartedly.

"I don't think we need to stand on ceremony tonight," Harry replied, winking. "We did bring you your clothes, so tomorrow you can shed those appalling pyjamas and look like yourself again."

Jack emerged from the hallway and took his place at the table. He didn't look at her. Harry poured him a glass of wine and held up his in a toast. "To lifelong friends." They all held their glasses to the light and Lillie watched Jack as he took an enormous swallow, draining nearly half his glass. He was upset, that was obvious, but so was she. They ate in silence for a few minutes.

Jack finally cleared his throat. "I went to the hospital today and poked around a little. It seems the fire was started outside Lillie's room. Intentionally. And I believe whoever started it killed the guard first and then torched the place."

"So he was murdered?" She was astonished. The poor man, and only doing his job. All this was because of her, because of them. If they hadn't been on this case that man would still be alive today.

"Yes, I think so."

"Did you find anything there? At the site?" Harry asked, smothering a piece of bread in butter.

"Only this." Jack dug into the pocket of his pants and pulled out the metal item he had been carrying around all day with him.

"What is that?" Harry asked, peering over the table to get a better look.

Lillie held out her hand. "May I?" Jack handed it to her, his fingers brushing hers. Lillie examined it, her face clouding over. "It can't possibly be...I don't understand..."

"What?" demanded Harry. "What is it?"

"It looks like..." she trailed off, rubbing at the front of it and trying to clean off the soot. "It's a lighter. And I have seen it before, at least I think I have...yes, I'm sure I have. You see, this picture, this sailboat? It belongs to Fitzherbert. I saw him with it a few months ago, in New York. Yes, I am certain—this is his lighter."

The silence in the room was at once deafening. The four of them sat staring at one another.

"He couldn't possibly be the one...why would he..." The words passed her lips and hung in the air, heavy and foreboding.

"You never really know someone, do you? Incidentally, how do you know this particular lighter is his, and there aren't many copies out there floating around." Harry said softly after a moment.

Lillie got up and paced the length of the room. "It has an 'F' underneath the sailboat. I noticed it at my sister's dinner party —I studied it because I remember being so annoyed that he was smoking that vile smelling cigarette, so I watched carefully as he lit it. This is impossible. Perhaps he dropped it when he was visiting someone in the hospital? Someone else?" She felt better making sense out of it.

"Yes, it's possible." Jack watched her from the table. "Possible, but the way it was found concerns me. Your guard had it clutched in his hand when he died, it was as though he wanted to make sure it was found. It makes this Fitzherbert a suspect, and as such we need to treat him with an abundance of caution."

Harry spoke up. "Or it could be that the guard started the fire with it himself."

"I doubt it, if he had, he would certainly not have been trapped or injured the way he was. I am sure he was killed because he tried to stop whoever was intent on starting it. I believe that person was likely this man you are speaking of."

"But he is my sister's husband's business associate. How could he be a murderer? It doesn't make any sense. Why would he want me dead? And what does this have to do with Lady

Swindon's death?" It was fleeting, but a flash of familiarity, a deeper knowing, a glint of comprehension even though the pieces didn't fit, seemed to hollow out a space in her thoughts. The park, her attack—something was...off.

"What is it?" Jack said, looking at her with concern.

"I....I remember something from my attack. The boots of the man who attacked me, they were—I mean, I had seen them before. In W. Franks, a specialty shop in New York. They make custom boots, very expensive ones. One would have to be in New York to get them, so a Londoner wouldn't have a pair—unless of course they had traveled to New York on a trip. But it would be unlikely, highly unlikely. Oh, I can't believe this!"

"What are you asserting?" Jack's face had clouded over.

"That those boots might have belonged to my brother-in-law."

"Yes, but have you actually ever seen Floyd wearing a pair of boots like that?" Primrose was ever the devil's advocate.

"Well..." Lillie said, thinking carefully. She put herself back in New York, tried to itemize Floyd's wardrobe. "Perhaps—but I can't be sure."

"There are too many coincidences here for my liking," Harry said.

"What if Floyd and Fitzherbert are in this together? Fitzherbert may also have been behind the murder of Hewitt Darcy, and definitely behind the murder of that poor guard who was at the hospital protecting me. Oh, I feel sick."

"Sit down." Jack guided her into a chair and poured her a large glass of whiskey from the sideboard.

"If our killer is Fitzherbert, either my brother-in-law knows and is aiding him, or he needs to be warned off. Either way, should I not try to get my sister away from him, at least until we can be sure? But how am I to do that?" Lillie wrapped her hand around her glass as though she was holding on for dear life.

"I doubt she is in any danger. He isn't randomly killing

people. If he is our man, he is methodical in his process and won't take the chance of making a mistake. He'll strike if he thinks he is close to being found out. What we need to do to secure your sister's safety is to project an image of normalcy. Under no circumstances can we let on to either your sister or to Floyd that we suspect him." Jack looked around the table at all three of them.

"Which means we can't stay holed up here in your flat forever. The longer we stay out of sight, the more dangerous things become for Lillie's sister," Primrose stated.

"I am afraid that is true, but we will need to take precautions. Under no circumstances is Floyd ever to get close to any of you—not without you being protected."

Lillie looked grim. "We tried for protection once, don't forget, and my guard was murdered."

"Yes, but the type of protection I have in mind will be a little different. There is one other thing: this business connection between your brother in law and this Mr. Fitzherbert?"

"Yes." Lillie said.

"What is it all about?"

"Gemstones, Fitzherbert has a gemstone mine in America. Red Emeralds."

"And, Mr. Fitzherbert has been seen in the company of not only Hewitt Darcy, but also Lord Swindon?"

"Correct." Harry had brought the article from the newspaper about Darcy's fall from the bridge. The picture was grainy, but Lillie had been fairly sure it was the same man she had seen dining with Lord Swindon and Fitzherbert at the Selfridges the day she and Primrose had gone shopping.

"I don't think we should ignore that London is a very large city, and that this Fitzherbert fellow is connected to at least three people who we know are tied to Lady Swindon's death in some way."

Harry spoke up. "And also, Lady Swindon owned an enormous Red Emerald gemstone that was given to her relatively recently."

"But just because Fitzherbert's company supplies Red Emeralds to the market doesn't mean there is a connection between Lady Swindon and him," Harry mused, more to himself than the room. He looked up. "Just think: there are thousands of diamond producers, but it doesn't mean there is a connection between one of them and a customer far down the production chain who happens to have a diamond bracelet."

"Diamonds aren't all that rare actually, contrary to popular belief. But Red Emeralds are very rare. They are only mined in one location in the world. Which means their scarcity is enormous—and Fitzherbert is one of the only purveyors. Plus, he sold directly to consumers without the assistance of a middle man, so my sister told me when we spent the afternoon together." Lillie added.

"So you believe there is a connection between the death of Lady Swindon and Mr. Fitzherbert?" Jack asked. "I confess, by the sounds of all this, I do, too."

"But you haven't asked the big question. *Why* would Fitzherbert want Lady Swindon dead?" Lillie asked. "It doesn't make sense. As far as we know, other than the existence of one of his gemstones in Lady Swindon's jewelry cupboard, there is no other connection between Fitzherbert and Lady Swindon. Don't you think we are reaching? And Floyd. Why would he become mixed up in all of this?" She didn't really need an answer, she already knew why—she flashed back to the memory of the horses being led out of the barn that morning in Manhattan—*money.*

Harry spoke next. "And how does Lord Swindon at Scotland Yard fit?"

"It is all just too confusing." Primrose looked desperate.

Jack said. "You are right. Very confusing. I think we should take steps to get some clarity. Our first order of business should be to take a little tour of the Red Emerald office and production facility. I assume it is either in London or nearby?"

Lillie nodded. "Yes, I believe Floyd was going to see it while he was here."

"Are we planning on walking unannounced through the front door?" Harry asked.

"I, not we," Jack said. "You and Primrose will go back to Claridge's in the morning, with a tail provided by my office, and have a long leisurely breakfast in the restaurant. Whoever has been following you will be pleased to see you show up again. You will have only been gone a day, for all they know you might have taken a sightseeing trip."

"How will you get into the Red Emerald offices?" Lillie asked.

"Under cover of night, and with a little device I have grown very fond of. It picks even the most conservative locks," Jack said, winking.

"I am coming with you," Lillie said sharply.

"Certainly not."

"It isn't open for discussion. If we aren't going to be seen, it shouldn't present any problem at all."

Jack rolled his eyes.

Harry laughed. "Good luck shaking her, old sport. She really is the most stubborn girl. When are you going in?"

Jack sighed. "Tomorrow night. Wish us luck." He glanced over at Lillie and held her gaze in mock seriousness. "Have you got anything to wear befitting a cat burglar?"

"Black is my colour," she retorted.

～

HARRY AND PRIMROSE retired to their respective rooms for the night, but Lillie was too wound up to sleep. She sat in the corner of the living room and watched Jack as he sipped his whiskey in the darkness of the room, with only the firelight to illuminate his elegant face.

"You don't need to sit way over there," he said without looking at her. "I don't bite and I promise I won't attempt to kiss you again."

She got up and moved closer to the fireplace. "Attempt to kiss me?" she asked. "I would say you did a pretty good job."

"But you hated it."

"I hated myself for not hating it," she replied truthfully.

"Ah, I see." He handed her his drink and she took a long sip, reflecting on the intimate gesture.

"I do want to thank you. I haven't said it properly. You saved my life, twice, and have given all three of us a safe haven here in your home. And you are helping us solve this convoluted case that I can't even begin to understand..."

"But you don't love me anymore." His voice was flat as he finished for her.

"I don't want to love you anymore, no."

"That isn't quite the same thing."

Lillie got up and walked over to the sofa he was sitting on. He opened his arms and moved so that she could sit curled up against his body. He lowered his face to the back of her neck and she could feel the electric brush of his lips on her skin.

"I can't live without you," he murmured into her hair.

"You have done a pretty good job of it until now."

"Not really. I have been with you for the past two years— you didn't realize it, of course, but I was."

Lillie pulled away from him, so she could read his face. "I don't really understand how you managed all of that."

"We have some 'capabilities', or rather, SIS does. At times, I would appropriate them for my personal use. It isn't really acceptable, and if my superiors found out I would be reprimanded. There, now I have told you all, and from this day forward I will have to stop or you may have me arrested."

Lillie giggled and watched the flames of the fire. "What type of 'capabilities'?"

Reluctantly, uncomfortably, he said, "Oh, this and that, a bit of letter reading, some listening here and there...never mind."

She sighed, his explanation no clearer than a storm cloud. "Why don't we just get to know one another again and see how it goes? I don't fully understand everything you have gone through, but I am glad you are here and alive. Whatever happens, we will always be friends."

His voice was rough as he replied, "I don't want to be your friend."

"Tell me something. How did you eventually realize Floyd was my brother-in-law and not my ex-fiancé?"

"It took some time. I had gone back across the channel after that night in Mayfair and then eventually on to Belgium as part of a clandestine unit. We were trying to gain a foothold there, essentially through civilian networks, gathering commercial and military intelligence."

"And to think I thought you were in France..." Lillie mused.

"I had to put everything I knew, my whole life, out of my head. We were Englishmen in extremely dangerous conditions, in hostile enemy territory. We had some success. By the end of the war I was traveling mostly to neutral countries in order to gain information, but eventually, in late 1918, I ended up in America."

Lillie shifted slightly. "Go on..."

Jack sighed, and then continued. "I knew your sister lived there, and I decided it was time to come out of the shadows. And perhaps, if I met her and explained, she could break things to you gently, more gently than I could anyway. I knew you were back there, through letters you had sent to Harry...." He paused, a guilt-riddled expression on his face, then continued, "I didn't know, at that time, that you weren't already married, your letters never said...anyway, I watched the house, for a while, as we spies tend to do. And then I saw Penny—she looks so much like you that for a moment I thought it *was* you. She was leaving the house, hand in hand with the same man you were dancing with, and then it all clicked." He stopped, put his face into his hands, and rubbed anxiously at his temples. "I couldn't believe how stupid I had been." His face wore a torn expression.

"So you just—*left*?" Anger simmered dangerously and Lillie fought hard to keep it down. "Just left me to believe and mourn your death?"

"I didn't know what to do—I was in New York on work. It was an operation that was quite lengthy and we had had the misfortune of already having lost two operatives. And there you were, unmarried, but I could hardly explain myself—and I shouldn't have been watching you..." He was stammering, his voice faltering, but she didn't care.

"How could you?" Her anger was rapidly dissolving and shifting into sadness, salted with a profound sense of nostalgic loss. Nothing would, nothing could, ever be the same again.

"I had to go back to England, there was no opportunity to explain. And then, time passed, and I heard of you moving on, and I..." Here he paused, finding the words. "I was afraid. I was afraid too much time had passed and you would hate me. I knew as long as you thought I was dead, somewhere in your heart you would still love me. It sounds ridiculous now, even to my ears." When he stopped speaking the silence in the room had the weight of finality. It hung suffocatingly around them.

She was finished sitting in his arms. A momentary lapse. She stood up. "I can't think about it any more tonight."

He reached out for her hand, his eyes locked on hers,

searching for something she wasn't prepared to give him. She pulled away.

Leaving the room, she heard him murmur behind her. "Please forgive me."

She didn't look back.

27

LILLIE

T HE RED EMERALD OFFICE WAS located in Hatton Garden on the edge of Farringdon Road. The area was well known for diamonds and gemstones, and so it was also infamous for having its fair share of jewelry heists and murders. The office would likely be quite secure as a result.

Lillie and Jack stood in the darkness at the back of a three-story, stone building located directly across the street from the Red Emerald office. They were clad from head to toe in black, only their faces white against the sliver of a moon.

Lillie shivered as Jack put his fingers to his lips and began to work on the lock of the large rusted steel door.

"Are you sure this is the easiest way in?" Lillie whispered anxiously, ignoring his command for silence. "It seems we should be picking the lock on the *actual* building we want to go in."

"You saw the blueprints yourself. This is where the network of underground tunnels begin, and there is no easier and safer way into a building than from underneath."

"I am slightly claustrophobic. I am not sure I can bore through a tunnel without having a panic attack."

Jack stopped what he was doing and looked at her. "Then you should wait here while I go in. I told you to stay at home," he reprimanded.

"I'll be fine," she said, more surely than she felt.

He got back to work and she heard a distinct click as the lock gave way. *Impressive*, she thought, reluctantly. He slowly pushed open the door and she winced as the hinges squeaked. They stepped inside the dark building, Lillie following closely behind as Jack navigated the corridors based on his memory of the architectural plans. She thought he must have a photographic memory, something she hadn't known about him, as he didn't falter once. As they descended down to the basement level, Lillie felt the air becoming colder and damper. She jumped as a rat scurried across their path, carrying something in its mouth.

"All right?" Jack looked back and squeezed her hand. She nodded, not feeling the least bit all right, but she needed to come to see the lab for herself—it was her case and she didn't want to miss anything.

They located the entrance to the tunnel and Lillie was relieved at its size. They would have to crouch, but thankfully they wouldn't have to crawl to get through it. The extensive network of catacombs were remnants of medieval priories fortified and expanded over the years by goldsmiths and jewelers to house and hide their fortunes. They were even rumoured to connect Ely Palace with Ye Olde Mitre and Bleeding Heart Yard. An entire subterranean world existed beneath the old seventeenth-century buildings above, and although dark and damp tonight, they provided the perfect cover. Lillie was unsure, however, of whether they were still passable.

Jack made quick work of the lock on the large hatch door, and before she knew it, they were making their way through the darkness under the street. She focused on her breathing and kept one hand on the back of Jack's coat, trying not to think about where they were or what they were doing. Soon, with the aid of Jack's handy work, they pushed through another locked hatch at the end of the tunnel and emerged into the basement of the Red Emerald building.

It was quiet and Lillie was relieved they hadn't happened upon a late night employee. They climbed the stairs to the main floor, which housed a large reception area and a series of offices radiating off from the center. The windows were large and the ceilings high, and even in the darkness Lillie could see how grand the main floor was. Business must be good to afford such a lavish space.

"Let's find the lab. We can search the office area later if we need to," Jack whispered.

"What are we looking for, exactly?"

"I don't know yet. Stay close."

They made their way through the reception area to a large set of sealed double doors. Through the half windows they could see beyond to a large industrial space housing long tables, microscopes, and sorting bins. A row of faceting machines lined the far wall, their overhead lights switched off for the night. The only incoming light was from the street lamps outside.

"I have the torch, but I think we can see enough without turning it on. I don't want to be seen from the street," Jack said.

They pushed through the unlocked doors and looked around the room. Each table had a series of bins on it. On the nearest table the gemstones in each bin were further divided by compartments and sorted by size and gradations of colour—lighter salmon-pink stones through dark blood-red ones. Lillie picked up a few, holding them up to the window for light.

"I can't see anything. I am going to need that torch you brought."

"Mind you don't keep it on for long," Jack said, pulling it from his coat pocket and handing it to her. "It needs rest periods to work properly—and be careful where you shine the light, the last thing we need is the police here."

Lillie switched it on and shone it on the stones she had in her hand.

"Hm, not as pretty as I would expect," she mused.

"In what way?" Jack asked absently as he began opening supply cupboards at the far end of the room, carefully searching each shelf.

"Well, they are sort of dirty looking, and scratched. Inside the stone, that is. And they have been faceted already, so they should look much nicer than a raw crystal would—but they don't. I certainly wouldn't buy one." She moved to the next bin, which held much larger gemstones. "These ones are even uglier. I don't understand—Lady Swindon's stone was much more beautiful than all of these. Perhaps there are only a very few quality stones and a whole bunch of lesser ones?"

Lillie started going from table to table trying to support her hypothesis. Each table held the same type of divided bins, with the same type of goods: terribly unattractive gemstones.

Lillie looked with confusion at Jack, who was busy going through the cupboards. "How can a company like Red Emerald make its investors rich, if all they have to sell are gemstones people wouldn't want to buy?"

Lillie moved over to the long table that held six faceting machines. To the left of each machine were small metal bins that held the raw hexagonal-shaped crystal in its natural state, and to the right were the finished products. All the newly faceted and polished stones—cushion cuts, pear shapes, round brilliants, trillions—were all tossed together, waiting to be sorted at the other tables. She imagined the bee-hive of activity in this room during business hours, faceters and sorters working side by side, the whir of the machines and the swish of busy fingers and eagle eyes sorting the thousands of tiny red stones. She ran her fingers through the gemstones as she would pebbles on a beach, turning them, shining her light, holding some closer to her face to inspect. None of them looked anything like the gem in Lady Swindon's necklace.

Lillie switched the torch off and Jack turned to look at her, apparently finding something in his search. He looked puzzled.

"Did you find something?"

"Normal things you would find in a cutting and sorting facility. Except this, that is." Jack held up a bottle filled with what looked like salt, a label with white type on the front announcing something she couldn't make out.

"What is that?"

"Radium bromide."

"Which is what, exactly?"

"Have you ever heard of Pierre and Marie Curie?"

"Vaguely. Why, what about them?" She remembered the name being mentioned at her sister's dinner party.

"They discovered this substance twenty odd years ago. It was once touted as a cure all for medical problems, although in recent years there have been a number of cases that have given pause for thought."

"In what way?"

"It is a dangerous substance to work with and can explode easily—but more importantly for us, it makes people very sick."

"Sick how?"

"General malaise, really, pallor, heart palpitations…"

"What about skin ulcerations? General anaemia?"

"Certainly, yes."

"Which are the conditions Lady Swindon had before she died."

Jack looked grim.

"Why would they have it here? I mean, what would its use be?"

"A chemist by the name of Crookes once used it to make a

very dull-looking diamond look much better. But that was ages ago—fifteen years at least."

"And these stones would very likely benefit from the same treatment, although I doubt it would fix serious structural flaws such as cracks and fissures."

"Perhaps not, but radiating the gemstones would give them a little more brilliance, and perhaps hide many of their negative traits." Jack gave her an apprehensive look and then resumed his inspection of the supply cupboard.

"There is another room..." she said, then trailed off, seeing Jack wasn't in a hurry to leave his search of the supply cupboard. Lillie made her way over to the non-descript door beyond the faceting table. She had almost missed it in the darkness and only noticed it because of its small, metal hinges which had caught the light of her torch. Otherwise, the door just looked like part of the wall.

The back room was much smaller than the main cutting and sorting lab and had no window. The middle of the room housed one square table with a series of suspended luminescent glass tubes. *What on earth?* They looked futuristic, their contents glowing in the darkness, each tube containing at least one red gemstone, some with many stones, all suspended in a phosphorescent gaseous compound. Lillie moved closer to have a look. The tubes and their contents were beautiful, like a snapshot from something not of this world.

"Radium bromide gas, I should think," Jack said from the doorway, startling her.

"How do you know?" She was across the room now, running her hand over the smooth glass of one of the tubes. She turned back to look at him. In the glowing light, he looked like an apparition, but she felt reassured by his presence.

"It glows just like that. During the war we had a small fleet of radioactive ambulances that had x-ray apparatuses on board.

Bloody dangerous compound. I can't believe they are using it in this environment."

"Look at this." Lillie pointed to one of the tubes, which contained a large red gemstone.

"Yes, as I thought. They are using the radium bromide to improve the appearance of their gems."

"I can't believe it. That's fraud, isn't it?"

"I would say so. But even more damning are the health implications for those women who are wearing the things."

"Like Lady Swindon," Lillie stated with gravity.

"Exactly. And there must be others out there with the same afflictions."

"Poisoned by radiation from the very gemstone her husband bought for her. You don't think he knew, do you?"

"Good question. He certainly knew Fitzherbert well enough to..." Jack broke off as they both heard the sound of a door opening and voices in the reception area. Jack put an anxious finger to his lips, motioned for her to follow, and slipped out through the door back into the cutting and sorting room.

Lillie quickly moved away from the glass tube she had had been touching, but as she did so, it fell from its housing and crashed onto the floor of the room. The gas dissipated, leaving two large, red stones on the tiles of the floor. Hurriedly, she kicked the broken glass and gemstones underneath the table and hid behind the door, holding her breath. She wondered if Jack had found a good hiding spot in the other room but didn't dare to go after him—the voices were getting louder and closer.

She waited, crushing herself against the wall. Lillie recognized one of the voices as Fitzherbert, but couldn't make out whom he was talking to. Their voices sounded tinny against the backdrop of an empty reception area. They got louder as they moved from the main hall into the cutting and sorting lab. Lillie's heart beat faster and she willed herself not to make a sound, as she was sure they must now be almost on top of Jack's hiding spot, wherever it was. He was probably in the supply closet.

"They haven't made the connection. Don't worry about it," came Fitzherbert's voice, sharp, but also tired.

"But they will, certainly. We need to move the radium off the premises. It shouldn't have been here in the first place." With a sickening realization, Lillie recognized the second voice as Floyd's. *And he knew about the radiation.* He wasn't just an oblivious investor—he was a willing accomplice.

"She hasn't even been seen since the fire." Fitzherbert again. "Which, incidentally, I should have been more careful starting. I thought it would kill her, and it obviously didn't." Lillie realized they were talking about her. *So, it was Fitzherbert who had tried to kill her—but more treasonously, Floyd seemed to know all about it!* Fitzherbert was still speaking. "Maybe she is on her way back to Oxford. A little fire can do wonders," he said, and laughed. "And where exactly are we to move it to? Your hotel room?"

"Don't be ridiculous. I am sure we can find an empty warehouse somewhere and continue there." Floyd sounded irritated.

"They can't prove anything. Even if they do prove she died of poisoning, they won't be able to track the source."

"You should have been more careful. Obviously a stone that size would absorb much more radiation than the smaller ones. We can get away with altering the melee, they are tiny enough, but the big ones are a gamble. This had better be a lesson to you. If this gets out, our share price will plummet and we will be finished."

"You have enjoyed quite a return on your investment at this point, haven't you?" Fitzherbert shot back. "I suggest you keep quiet and let me run this operation. I certainly don't need any input from you."

Floyd grunted his displeasure. "So? What do you want to show me?"

"This way." The sound of their voices grew louder as they headed toward the radiation room. Realizing one housing stand was now empty of its glass tube, she leapt forward and grabbed the stand from the table, clasping it tightly in her hand as she again crushed herself behind the door.

Stay still, she willed herself silently. *Don't breathe until they are gone.*

"I don't need to see it any closer up," she heard Floyd say as the door was pushed open, crowding her body behind it. The two of them were close enough that she could smell their cologne and even a hint of garlic from their dinner. She felt a slow trickle of sweat travel down the side of her body from under her arm. "Very impressive."

"Glad you like it. Trust me, the only way this venture will stay profitable is to have these stones radiated. They just aren't marketable otherwise."

"I still worry about the connection we have to Lady Swindon's death. I know Lillie. If she gets a whiff of it, she will do everything in her power to bury us. Don't forget, she has all the press behind her—especially with the *London Telegraph* and the *Herald* picking up the stories. It could be disastrous for us."

"The most logical solution is still to pin this on Lord Swindon. Spurned husband and all that. We can expose that affair with the Irishman and use it to our advantage. Just takes a bit of imagination is all." Fitzherbert sounded confident.

"Have a Lord convicted for the murder of his wife? Might be a great deal more difficult than you imagine."

"Perhaps, but not impossible."

The two men made their way back into the reception area and Lillie let out a nervous exhale.

She stayed where she was, assuming Jack was still holed up in the storage cupboard, waiting. She wanted to be absolutely sure the men were gone. A minute later, the door to the radiation room was pushed open again and Jack's hand silently reached around and clasped her wrist, pulling her out from her hiding spot. Carefully, silently, they slowly made their way out of the lab and back the way they came. They descended the stairs to the basement and Lillie waited as Jack negotiated the hatch to the tunnel. Neither of them spoke. They emerged minutes later out the back of the building across the street from Red Emerald and retrieved Jack's motorcycle from the dilapidated shed they had hid it in.

It wasn't until she was on the back and they were moving at speed through the dark streets of London that Lillie felt relief. She wrapped her arms tighter around Jack's waist and rested her head on his back. He reached back with one hand and gave her leg a squeeze. They were safe. For now.

28

"WE NEED TO GET MY SISTER away from that psychopath immediately." Lillie paced the length of Jack's living room. "He actually *gave* her one of those necklaces—I saw it when I met her at her hotel a few days ago. If we are right, and Lady Swindon was poisoned by her own necklace, my sister is in grave danger."

"I agree with you. But we are going to need some time to figure out the best way to do that," Jack said. "Harry sent an update. They are indeed being watched and he is thinking of taking Primrose back to Oxford on the first train. He believes that will remove them from the equation and make them less of a target. I think they should go, and take Rumple with them."

"And Constable Worley?"

"He could be a help to us. I don't think anyone realizes he is working with us and he is at least trained in this sort of thing."

"As opposed to me?" Lillie looked frustrated and hurt, but Jack knew she mostly just needed a good night's sleep.

He looked at her and thought again how beautiful she was, and how much he had missed her. He didn't answer, knowing anything he said wouldn't appease her.

"Jack?" She was prompting him, or needling him, he wasn't sure.

"Go to bed—you are tired. We both are. I promise you in the morning we will formulate a plan to help your sister."

"I can't sleep." She was petulant, but also determined.

Jack walked over to her and took her hand and led her into his bedroom. She didn't protest. He sat her down on the bed and began to remove her shoes.

"I can do that," she snapped.

"Shush, you are being very rude."

She frowned at him.

He playfully pushed her down onto the bed and stood up. "Go to sleep," he told her. "We did a good job tonight."

Lillie lay back on top of the covers and let out a sigh. "You really irritate me."

"Is that so?" Jack leaned over her and kissed her forehead. He willed himself to leave the room, although it was the very last thing he wanted to do. What he really wanted to do was crawl under the covers with her, something he had never done. As he closed the door, he thought he heard her whisper his name. He looked back, but she was fast asleep.

JACK COULDN'T SLEEP in the end. He spent a few restless hours tossing and turning but eventually gave up, deciding instead to make a ludicrously strong pot of coffee. As he started in on his third cup, Lillie emerged from the bedroom and sat down across the table from him. Jack poured her a cup and mixed the cream and sugar in for her. They drank in silence for a few minutes. The morning light hadn't yet broken.

"I have a plan," he finally said.

"Do tell." She put her cup down.

"We get your sister on that train this morning with Harry and Primrose."

"Sounds perfect, but how?"

"You are going to telephone her and ask to meet at the cafe down the road from the hotel. We can assume Floyd will have her followed. When she sits down, I will have a waiter give her a message asking to meet you by the ladies' room. She will go to the back of the cafe and I will have an operative there who will whisk her out the back way to the safety of the train to Oxford. By the time Floyd realizes she is gone and not just powdering her nose, she will be at the train station."

"What time should I be at the cafe?"

"Don't be ridiculous—it is just a cover. I am not putting you in harm's way."

"But Penny will be terrified if some strange man tries to take her out of there. She will think she is being kidnapped."

Jack had anticipated this, but he didn't have an answer for it.

Lillie said, "No, I will go and I can accompany her to the station. She won't believe any of it unless it comes from me, and even then..."

Jack held his hands up in surrender. "All right, but it has to be executed perfectly. I can't fully predict how attentive Floyd will be. I will be waiting at the station with Harry and Primrose. I want to be absolutely sure the train is held in case you are late with Penny. You will be with my operative at all times. Do you understand?" Lillie nodded. "Okay, finish your coffee and have something to eat. Then let's get ready to go."

29

L ATER THAT MORNING, JACK dropped Lillie a few blocks down the street from the cafe he had chosen for the rendezvous. The operative was waiting.

"Marcel, this is Lillie. Lillie, Marcel." Jack could see Lillie was surprised how small of stature he was. "Marcel is the best in his field, came to us from France, former SCR. But now he works for us. He is doing me a favour on this, though. *Oui, mon ami?*"

Marcel smiled and nodded.

"Okay, you both know the plan. Penny should be there within the half hour—you better get going." Jack looked at Lillie, suddenly noticing her sickly pallor and glazed eyes. "You don't look very well, are you feeling all right?"

"Fine, yes. Just a little tired," she answered, but her voice sounded weak and distracted.

Jack wasn't so sure.

"Perhaps I should be the one waiting for Penny," he said, not liking her abrupt downturn. He noticed she was sweating slightly across her forehead.

"No, no. She has never met you—not in person anyway. She

may recognize you from old photographs I have shown her, but that would just raise more questions than we have time for today. She won't trust you. It has to be me." Just the act of speaking the words seemed to be sapping her strength.

Jack looked at her and reluctantly conceded. At least is would be over soon and he would be with her again within the hour. If she was coming down with something, it could hardly worsen in that short a time frame.

Marcel nodded to Jack and they parted ways. As he walked away, Jack had a sinking feeling that something wasn't right. He looked back, beginning to have a change of heart, but they were gone.

30

LILLIE

T HE CAFE WAS MORE OF A BISTRO and less of a coffee shop. Lillie had expected a casual atmosphere, but instead the small room was elegantly defined by simple, round, marble-topped tables and woven art-nouveau chairs which were clustered haphazardly throughout the room. The walls were painted a deep shade of red and she noticed listlessly that pictures of Paris in expensive, mismatched frames —some sketches, some watercolours—were hung with no particular thought or order.

She really *wasn't* feeling well. Perhaps it was a sudden onset of the flu. Or the lack of sleep. The past few nights she hadn't slept for more than about three hours in total. Whatever it was, it felt like she had been hit by a train. The lopsided pictures on the wall were making her feel woozy.

She looked at the operative Jack had installed as her bodyguard. He was shorter than she was, had the body of a runner —thin but strong—and wore small round spectacles that made him look as though he had just emerged from sorting books in the local library. He was studying her now, a look of concerned dissatisfaction on his face.

"Something is wrong, no?" Marcel asked in heavily accented English.

"A great deal." She was referring to everything they had discovered in the last day and trying to ignore the fact she had begun sweating beneath her coat.

"I mean with your health."

"Not at all. I am fine," she lied.

Marcel nodded, still looking dissatisfied. He motioned wordlessly to the back of the cafe, and then slipped off, leaving her alone.

Fighting a new, surprising urge to collapse, Lillie did as Jack had instructed her to do: find a small table near the front of the restaurant. Sit down. Order a cup of tea. She waited the prescribed time of five minutes, then gave the waitress a description of her sister, asked her to seat her at the table, and hand her the note Lillie had hastily written. Then she got up, leaving her untouched tea on the table, and made her way towards the restroom.

As expected, Marcel wasn't anywhere to be seen. Lillie stationed herself in a small alcove off the hallway by the restroom, used as a coatroom. It was currently full of wet coats and had a peculiar smell of damp dog and cheap perfume. She fought the urge to vomit. From her vantage point, she could just barely see the front door to the café, but had a perfect view of the entire dining room. She waited for Penny's arrival.

Thankfully, it came just a few minutes later, her sister rushing through the door, trailing a sharply-dressed, and annoyed looking Floyd behind her. They had expected he would come, which complicated things, but it wasn't insur- mountable. As she watched him hover over her sister, she thought back to the previous evening with mounting anger— her body crushed behind the door of the lab, his voice confirming he had knowledge of who started the fire that had

almost killed her, the sickening smell of his cologne. The
bastard.

They took their seats at the table and the waitress handed
Penny the note, which instructed her to tell Floyd Lillie was
running late, and to excuse herself to go to the restroom. Lillie
watched her sister's face, praying she would do as instructed
and not give anything away to her husband, who was sitting
across from her and saying something Lillie couldn't hear. She
watched as Penny discreetly folded the letter and slipped it into
her purse. She smiled at her husband—a smile only a sister
would know wasn't genuine—and excused herself.

So far, so good.

Lillie lost sight of Penny as she left the table, but thankfully
Floyd remained seated and didn't follow her. They wouldn't
have much time once Penny met her. If they were to escape
Floyd's clutches, her sister would have to believe Lillie immediately without question or hesitation and they would have to
make their way to the car waiting for them out back. Marcel
was, hopefully, already installed at the wheel.

Lillie could hear the clack of shoes on the parquet floor
outside her hiding spot. Her sister had a distinct gait—quick
and efficient—and Lillie reached out and pulled her towards
her, putting a finger to her lips to silence any protest.

"Lillie! Oh, thank God you are all right. I have been so
worried about you, since the fire at the hospital...."

"Shhh, later...." There wasn't enough time. Her hands were
clammy, the air was too warm, and they needed to move.
"Listen to me. Floyd is dangerous. You don't know what he is
really up to, Penny. He is involved in a plot to kill me. You need
to come with me now. I can explain it all in time, but he can't
know we are leaving." She started pulling Penny down the
hallway with her towards the kitchen. Beyond that lay the door
to the back alley and Marcel.

"What on earth are you talking about? Lillie? This is ridiculous. Are you alright? You look sick." She was scurrying along quickly, trying to keep up. "I don't know why you think—" Lillie cut her off. "Believe it. He is not what you think. We have to go, now." Why was she resisting? It was hard enough to get away without having to physically drag her.

"Your hands, they are so hot! Lillie, you don't look—" A voice behind them, raised and icy, stopped her in her tracks. "Let go of her!" Floyd commanded.

Lillie looked back to see him standing in the hallway. He had a look on his face that frightened her, and obviously Penny felt the same way, because she gave Lillie a little nudge. *Forward...keep going.* Her sister believed her—perhaps she had suspected all along, on some subconscious level. Lillie tried to quicken her pace.

They had reached the doors of the kitchen. Lillie felt her sister's fingers on her back, pushing her. *Keep running,* she told herself. He couldn't very well stop them in a public place and hold them against their will. The women pushed through the doors to the kitchen. At least five stunned faces greeted them. The chefs and their kitchen staffers stood frozen in the midst of their lunch duties, knives carefully placed on the counter in front of them, sauces boiling over on the stove behind. They watched the scene unfolding before them in utter disbelief. Lillie knew even before Floyd spoke behind her, even before she saw Marcel's unconscious body on the floor to the left of the kitchen doors, that they hadn't planned for all eventualities.

"Stop now or I will shoot," came a voice she recognized from behind a partition wall.

That explained the looks on the faces of the kitchen staff. They should have realized Floyd would not only follow Penny, but bring reinforcements with him.

Lillie swivelled her head to the right and found she was

staring directly into the stout, cold barrel of a gun. It was aimed unwaveringly at her forehead. Two dark, almost black eyes, underneath which had a mouth set in a grim, determined line, stared back at her.

31

J ACK ARRIVED AT THE TRAIN station twenty minutes after leaving Lillie and Marcel at the cafe. He found Harry in front of the newsagent's stand in the spot they had agreed upon.

"Where is Primrose?" he asked Harry.

"Just picking up a few essentials in the shop across the way. I didn't want her out of my sight, but I knew you would have a heart attack if I weren't where I'd promised to be."

"Thanks. I am a bit on edge with this whole thing. Lillie has gone to get Penny, but I am worried about her. I think she is coming down with something. She doesn't look well at all."

"I wouldn't worry, old chap," Harry said, smiling. "She has been through a lot the last few days. Those attempts on her life are sure to have wreaked havoc with her immune system."

"True. Listen, are you all ready to go? You might be running to catch that train if our timing isn't perfect."

"I am. Rumple has the luggage and is waiting on the platform now. I asked Constable Worley to join him. Worley wants to get home anyway and it can't hurt to have some reinforcements in case Penny is followed. I think the sooner we get out of this city the better. You don't think we will be followed to Oxford?"

"If they realize where we are going then I think, yes, we will likely be in their sights. Especially now we are taking Penny with us. Best thing is to lie low for a while, at least until I can have Scotland Yard arrest Fitzherbert and Floyd and wind this thing up. It shouldn't be long. We have the evidence against them and it won't be difficult to put two and two together and determine the source of the poison in Lady Swindon's death."

"Amazing, isn't it? Radiation poisoning from the very necklace her husband gave her as a gift on her birthday. There they were, trying to put the past behind them. And now she is dead. Not to mention all the other women out there wearing these irradiated gemstones around their necks."

"I guess when this Fitzherbert realized his gemstone was the likely source of Lady Swindon's poisoning, he sent his thug to bribe Worley to close the case." Harry reached inside a bag he was holding and retrieved a scone, offering one to Jack.

"Looks like it," Jack said, waving it away. He was too wound up to eat.

"Do you think Lord Swindon had some inkling of this?" Harry said as he chewed, his face thoughtful. Jack envied his friend's ability to compartmentalize his feelings and not let anything interfere with a meal or a drink. Or perhaps Harry had just never been given much cause to worry, and as such, it was a foreign concept to him.

"I think so. That must have been why you saw him at Scotland Yard. Probably trying to get the police to investigate the lab. It can take some time to get a search warrant though—one has to be pretty convincing."

"Good thing you can pick a lock better than a thief and aren't hampered by tedious bits of paper. This case could have gone on forever."

Jack smiled at Harry and winked.

"Tell me, what are your plans now that your secret spy life is out in the open?"

"I hadn't really thought. Some of our operatives are married, so it isn't unheard of to have a life. I should like to have a wife and children one day, I suppose. Perhaps a flat in the city and a house in the country with a rambling rose bush at the front door, a lake out back, and miles of fields to walk through."

"Sounds to me as though you have given it some thought, old sport. A great deal of thought. And Lillie?"

"I hope to persuade her to stay in England. I won't lie—I hope I can persuade her to marry me. It might take some time though. She is certainly trying to keep her distance."

The two men watched as Primrose emerged from the shop and made her way over to them.

"All ready! Any sign of Lillie and Penny?" Primrose was breathless and anxious.

"Not yet. Let's get to the platform and find Rumple. It won't be long before the train arrives." Harry relieved Primrose of her bag and took hold of her hand.

"I'll stay here and watch for them. You get ready." Jack nodded, dismissing them.

As he made his way back onto the sidewalk in front of the station to take up his watch, Jack thought to himself, *Everything should be in motion now.*

But a feeling of dread washed over him. Although he couldn't pinpoint what it was, something felt horribly wrong.

32

LILLIE

THE THING ABOUT A GUN IS: IT'S only as dangerous as the person operating it. Unfortunately for Lillie and Penny, the person holding this one was a man with nothing left to lose.

The now immobilized chef and his sous chefs looked like figurines an organized child had placed on a shelf to play with after dinner. Each one in a white uniform, hands by their sides, mouths set in a line. Only the darting of their pupils humanized them.

Out of the corner of her eye, Lillie could see Marcel still slumped on the floor. Was he dead? She couldn't see any blood, but he was certainly unconscious. She thought she saw a slight movement of his left hand, but perhaps it was her imagination. The sound of Penny breathing behind her, and the realization that at any moment the man holding the gun might shoot them all, kept her alert enough to stop her collapsing on the floor beside Jack's operative. Her legs felt like rubber. A steady drip of sweat ran down her back. Her head pounded and she began to notice black spots in her vision. How much longer could she remain conscious?

She stared back at the face of the man holding their lives in the balance. She should have seen it earlier, she should have seen signs, she should have seen *something that told her Edgar was involved.* He had seemed so distraught over his mother's death and now here he was, in this kitchen, months later, part of the whole mess.

Edgar's face looked as though it had been carved of ice. "Get moving," he commanded. "Out to the alley." He motioned in the direction of the rear exit with the barrel of the gun.

Lillie stayed planted where she was. "So it's you, is it?" She stated flatly, feeling heat creep into her face, and fighting the urge to lay down. "How could you possibly have killed your own mother?"

Edgar's face clouded over. "It wasn't intentional."

"No? Well, this certainly is." Lillie pointed to the gun.

"I didn't know anything about radium bromide—only that they made the stones look better. My father introduced me to the company, and when Fitzherbert hired me, my poor mother was our first big sale. That necklace you saw in her cabinet at Wrenhaven was a fortune. Had I known everything, I would never have sold it to her."

"And now?"

"When mother died I realized I was in trouble. I'm not a Swindon, my father was an Irishman—some man my mother had an affair with. Do you really think I would be heir to the Swindon fortune? Upon her death, I realized I had nothing in the world except this job. I need it, and this is just a means to an end now."

"You don't have to do this," Lillie was pleading for their lives. "It will only get worse and worse for you. You can go to the police, tell them what you have told me!" Lillie thought of what Harry had told her about seeing Lord Swindon at Scotland Yard. He must have suspected Edgar.

Edgar gave her a sad smile. "It's too late. I'm all in now, I'm afraid." He waved the butt of the gun towards the back door of the kitchen. "Time to go."

Floyd ushered Penny along and she bumped into the back of Lillie, nearly knocking her over. Doing as she was told, Lillie cast a final, mournful glance at Marcel on the floor, and walked toward the back of the kitchen. What was next? Where were they going to take them? She was certain they wouldn't let them live long.

Emerging into the sharp light of day, Lillie quickly assessed her surroundings. The alley was about two hundred feet long. The brick buildings that lined it were windowless on this side, and their alley entrances served as commercial delivery points for the various restaurants and shops that fronted the prestigious avenues on the other side. In front of them was the car Marcel had brought, a dark-navy Packard with an ebony roof. Beyond it was another car she didn't recognize, a small Irish-green convertible that looked sportier and faster than their own. In the distance she could see a couple of homeless men, a small fire pit in front of them, watching the scene unfold as they rubbed their hands over the flames. One of them got up slowly, limping, and seemed to be winding his way towards them to get a closer look. He wore the run-down clothing of a vagabond, but had three medals pinned to his lapel. Was he insane? Had he not seen the gun?

Neither Floyd nor Edgar had noticed the man, both focused instead on getting the girls into the sports car. As they pushed and prodded them like cattle, Lillie slipped on the threshold of the car and fell to the ground, cutting her already bruised face on the metal. Blood spilled onto the ground and she lay still for a moment, her head reeling.

Floyd rushed forward and kicked her in the ribs. "Get up!"

Lillie rolled over and vomited all over his shoes.

She heard Penny cry out and watched from the ground as

her sister spun around and struck Floyd hard in the head with her purse, knocking him off balance. In an instant the scene unfolded into a blur of thrashing arms and yelling. The man in the alley had reached them now and, to Lillie's utter shock, catapulted himself like a cat onto Edgar's back. The two men spun around, gun dangling dangerously from Edgar's fingers, as he tried desperately to shake the load off his back. The homeless man, in an act of bravery befitting a decorated veteran, completely disregarded his own safety, and wrapped one moth-eaten wool arm around Edgar's neck and squeezed unrelentingly. Turning an unpleasant shade of purple, Edgar fell to the ground, dropping the gun onto the cobblestones. They all watched as it went skidding under the car with a clatter. Floyd, recovering slightly, pushed Penny aside and scrambled under the car to retrieve it.

At that moment, the back door of the cafe was flung open with a clang and Marcel burst onto the scene as though he had been launched out of a cannon. With a swift kick to the head, he ended Edgar's struggle with the homeless soldier, and in the same movement, grabbed hold of Floyd's ankles and dragged him from underneath the car. Clutching the back of his coat, he handily swung Floyd around—an amazing feat given the size difference—and punched him squarely in the jaw, once very hard, and then twice more for good measure. Floyd hit the ground, and stayed there.

Standing up and straightening his glasses, Marcel nodded an efficient thanks towards the veteran, who smiled at them, brushed off his medals with one dirty hand, and limped back off in the direction he had come. Penny helped Lillie off the ground, and half holding her up, pushed her towards Marcel's car and into the back seat.

"Hurry!" Marcel urged. "They won't be down forever, and we need to make that train!"

Lillie heard the car door slam and the firing of shots as they roared down the alley and headed towards Paddington Station. Only the cool of the leather seat on her bruised cheek and the taste of blood in her mouth kept her teetering on the edge of consciousness.

I T WAS ANOTHER AGONIZING FORTY-five minutes before Jack saw Marcel's navy-blue car pull up to the front doors of the train station. He rushed out to meet it, glancing at the clock as he did so. The train was in the station and would be leaving shortly. Jack flung open the rear car door and grabbed a surprised Penny's hand.

"Who are you?" she exclaimed.

"Jack Abbott, I'll explain later. We haven't a minute to lose."

Marcel had Lillie's door open and was pulling her half-conscious body out of the car, propping her up and urging her to walk. Jack watched in horror as blood dripped onto the lapel of her coat from a gash on her cheek.

"Jack, she isn't at all well," he said quickly.

Jack wrapped an arm around Lillie's waist as she sagged against him.

"Marcel," Jack commanded. "Take Penny to platform four right away."

"No! I can't leave my sister like this!" Penny cried.

Jack held his hand to Lillie's forehead. It was clammy, but hot. She looked up at him blankly, her eyes glassy. "Listen to me, change of plans—I am going to carry you and we are going to get on that train to Oxford. Do you understand?"

He swung her up into his arms and hurried through the station. When they reached the platform, the train was whistling its last call and the porters were shutting the doors.

"Jack!" Harry called, waving to him from the carriage.

Rumple stood at attention on the platform, waiting for them. Another man who Jack assumed must be Worley stood a few feet away, scanning the crowd. Jack was relieved see the giveaway bumps of firearms under the fabric of their coats.

They all moved quickly into the car Harry had reserved and as the train gave its final whistle, Jack heard Penny's name being shouted from farther down the platform. He looked back to see Floyd running the length of the station. Penny covered her ears as the train edged away from the station. Floyd managed to locate her window and grabbed the sill, his face full of fury. Rumple calmly stood up, walked over to the open window, and put his gun to Floyd's forehead. Stunned, Floyd stopped running. Still clutching at the window, his feet dragged along the platform with a hideous scraping sound until he finally had the good sense to let go. Rumple calmly pulled the window closed and patted Penny on the shoulder.

The train gathered speed as it left the station behind. The only sound in the car was that of Penny weeping.

EPILOGUE

A MONTH LATER

LILLIE

"I AM GETTING MARRIED," HARRY announced, folding the newspaper he had been reading and placing it in his lap.

"Oh no, Harry, I don't think you should. Beatrice isn't going to make you happy, that much is obvious. I thought you vowed not to listen to your mother anymore? Trust me—you will be miserable with that girl." Lillie frowned at him across the Tynesmore drawing room.

It was nice to be feeling better, but after a month, she still wasn't well enough to venture outside. She had redirected her focus inside the house, which had been decorated, every square inch, in celebration of Christmas tomorrow. Harry had the most childlike love of the holiday and she and Rumple had spent days trimming the house for him.

"Not to Beatrice, you silly girl. To Primrose."

"Oh!" Lillie gasped and then laughed. "To Primrose, how delightful! But she hasn't said a thing to me! I always knew you two were perfect for each other."

"She didn't want to tell you until you were back to your normal self, but I selfishly couldn't wait any longer. Honestly, you have taken this whole radiation poisoning thing to a new level. Only you could become deathly ill from breaking into a gemstone lab."

"It hasn't quite been a picnic for me either, Harry."

"You haven't had to put up with Jack. He has been beside himself with worry. I don't think we could have had any more specialists here over the last month. He brought them from all over England and Europe to see you. Every night I had to make dinner conversation with some frighteningly intelligent doctor with a vocabulary that made me feel as though I had never attended school. It is amazing Primrose doesn't look at me now and think I am a buffoon."

"Your ruse is up, is it?"

"At least I have my looks. Those shouldn't fade for a few years anyway."

"I am so pleased for you both. When is the wedding?"

"Soon. I don't want to give her a chance to change her mind. Perhaps January, if I can get the arrangements made in time."

Lillie gave him a doubtful look.

"Or February—" he conceded, with reluctance. "Incidentally, have you noticed how close Penny and Rumple have become?" Harry had a twinkle in his eye. "I know Penny thinks of him as a big brother, but I am not sure of Rumple's intentions."

"I can see that. It is good for both of them. I can imagine Penny is having a difficult time coming to grips with Floyd's treachery. She told me yesterday she would like to stay in Oxford."

The door to the drawing room opened and in strode Jack, his cheeks flushed from the chill outside.

"Who is staying in Oxford?" he asked as he leaned over Lillie's chair and kissed her forehead. He had taken to being very bold with his affections of late, not caring who was in the room to see them. She didn't really mind. In fact, she was secretly pleased that he was so obviously in love with her.

"I was just telling Harry that Penny has decided to stay in Oxford for a while. She doesn't want to return to New York until after everything is settled with her divorce. That could take some time now that Floyd is on trial with Fitzherbert for murder and fraud, not to mention the assault and attempted kidnapping. It looks as though Edgar will be tried in Oxford. It could take ages to wrap it all up. However, I don't think we can stay here at Tynesmore much longer, since soon you will have your new bride here." She winked at Harry.

"Don't be ridiculous. You may stay as long as you like. I hear old Jeremy Winston from the newspaper wants you back at work. That final column you wrote while you were recovering resulted in the most popular edition of the Oxford Daily Press since its inception," Harry said, holding up the newspaper and stabbing his finger at an article on the front page. "Perhaps when you accept you could set to work on solving this case—a body found in north Oxfordshire yesterday. It appears the man was stabbed—"

Lillie held her hand up to silence him. She hadn't wanted to discuss her plans in front of Jack just yet, and now he had gone and spilled everything.

Jack looked startled at the news. "You can't be serious. Lillie, you were attacked in a London park, barely emerged from a fire, and suffered radiation poisoning which, may I remind you, you almost died from! I think a change of career might be in order."

"Jack, you must know that if you tell me to do something, I will most certainly do the opposite. And you are a spy, for goodness' sake. You can hardly criticize my career path. And further to that, I am seeing a house later today, for Penny and me."

"I don't understand." Jack looked bewildered.

"To live in. If we are staying in Oxford, we must have a place of our own. It is a cottage really, but quite pretty. I asked Rumple to drive me by it yesterday. It has some land and a vegetable garden and three bedrooms. It is for let, but I believe I could purchase it if we like it. I have my trust, my father left me plenty of money, so that shouldn't be an issue."

Jack sat in the chair beside her and reached for hand. "But I thought you would perhaps live with me one day," he said tenderly.

Lillie smiled at him, but didn't answer. Although she was coming to terms with how he had left her, she still didn't know if she would ever be able to trust him again. At least enough to spend her life with him.

Harry spoke. "A woman buying a house of her own. What is this world coming to?"

"It is changing, Harry, and hopefully for the better." Lillie squeezed Jack's hand and looked at him. "Would you like to come with me to see the cottage this afternoon? I would like your opinion."

"Of course. You couldn't keep me away."

"Good." Lillie smiled at him. "And incidentally, Jack Abbott, I hope you never go away again."

"I believe you are stuck with me," Jack said triumphantly.

There was a knock on the drawing room door and Rumple ceremoniously entered the room, wearing an astonishing crimson, velvet cape that was easily long enough to trip on, dark-brown, laced boots and black, calf-length pants. His ensemble was topped with a ruffled white blouse reminiscent of something a king would adorn. He was carrying an absurdly large, silver tray with a variety of miniature tarts and cakes and was demurely followed by a hall boy. He was pushing a table-clothed rolling cart on which was set a selection of glass mugs, each decorated with a glittering snowflake, and a bubbling cauldron of hot mulled wine.

"And who might we be expecting, Father Christmas?" Harry raised an inquisitive eyebrow. "I think you have enough alcohol there for an entire naval regiment—a Russian one, at that."

"Lord Swindon, the elder, and the charming Ms. Penny Mead." Since the incident on the train Rumple had taken to dropping Penny's married name and addressing her by her maiden name. "Also, sir, Jeremy Winston telephoned earlier to request a visit with the patient. I tried to put him off, but he really is the most assertive man—terribly unbecoming. Certainly *not* the behaviour of a gentleman." He nodded at the three of them and, with a swish of his cape, exited the room.

Harry looked up to the heavens.

Lillie, stifling a giggle, carefully got up from the comfortable chair in which she had been spending far too much time lately. Her entire body felt the stiffness that came with days of inactivity. Her strength wasn't what it had been before the incident in the lab when she'd broken the radium bromide container and poisoned herself, but it was coming steadily back, day by day. She wandered over to the Christmas tree she and Rumple had finished trimming that afternoon—a magnificent Fraser fir that smelled of a snow coated forest. She brushed her fingers over its soft needles and marvelled at its staggering height. Originally she had thought it better suited to the grand hallway, but Rumple had insisted it should be erected where she could enjoy it from the comfort of her chair. It had taken some man-handling and a broken sixteenth century vase to get it into the room, but she appreciated the effort now as she inhaled its scent and admired its glittering baubles.

The door to the drawing room opened again and, with a dash of reluctance sure to please Jack, Rumple announced Jeremy's arrival.

"Well, I am very glad to see you on your feet." Jeremy rushed forward and gave Lillie an embrace that, by the look on Jack's face, irritated him. Lillie carefully pulled away, not letting the moment linger.

"Have a seat, old chap," Harry called from his chair, nose buried in the newspaper again. "Mulled wine?"

"No, thank you. I haven't long. I just came to see how Lillie's recovery is going and to talk a little shop, if she doesn't mind."

"Not at all." Lillie glanced towards Jack, who was frowning intently at Jeremy as he poured himself a drink. The smell of cinnamon and orange filled the air.

"I wanted to offer you the lead position on the crime desk at the newspaper. Now I realize you haven't had much time to adjust to how we do things, and this case has been terribly—well, downright dangerous, actually."

From Jack came a loudly dissatisfied and obvious *hmph*.

Jeremy glanced in his direction. "Right. Well, anyway, you would be responsible for overseeing the other reporters' work, and, of course, still writing your own column. Your mandate would include *you* deciding what we choose to investigate and report on and how we do it. I'm willing to hire another couple of reporters to work under your tutelage."

"I should be delighted, Jeremy. Thank you for the opportunity—and I have to tell you, I think we have our next story already. There's a body that's just been found in North Oxfordshire—"

Lillie shot Jack a warning glance as he started to open his mouth to speak. He wisely shut it again and glared at Jeremy instead, angrily taking a large gulp of mulled wine.

"Right, then that's our next focus if you are up for it?"

Lillie nodded her agreement.

"Good, that is settled. Start as soon as you can. Merry Christmas, everyone." He nodded to Jack and Harry and took his leave.

Rumple swished ahead of him, his cape narrowly missing a priceless set of glass figurines Harry had brought back from London, and held the door open for Jeremy.

Lead crime reporter. It had a nice ring to it. Lillie smiled to herself. First order of business was to secure that little cottage she had fallen in love with. She would not be returning to New York. It was decided.

"Lord Swindon and Ms. Penny Mead to see you," Rumple announced, standing at the door, stick-straight, as though slouching were considered a capital offence. He nodded dismissively to the backside of Jeremy and executed a charming smile for Penny as she entered the room. Lillie supposed Rumple was beginning to have a little crush on her sister and she wondered absently if Rose, the cook, had noticed yet. She hoped not.

"Welcome!" Harry boomed, getting up from his chair and abandoning the newspaper. "Rumple, drinks all around."

"What a beautiful tree," Penny said, looking up at the fir with amazement. She accepted a mug of wine.

"It certainly is," Lord Swindon agreed, sipping his drink, and seemingly in better spirits than Lillie had ever seen him. "I finally agreed to decorate Wrenhaven for Christmas this year, as well. I confess, the thought of the holiday season without the usual trappings of Christmas had me downcast. But I have you to thank for giving us our optimism back. Solving Eleanor's case has been a real weight off my shoulders," he said, with a sorrowful smile. "I admit I am terribly sad about Edgar's part in the whole thing, although after some deep soul-searching, I can't help but admit I have played a part. I shouldn't have pushed him so hard, professionally. He somehow thought he wouldn't be my heir, and I never reassured him otherwise—I should have."

A silence descended, and the air held a suspended sombreness.

Harry quietly gulped down the rest of his drink and Rumple swooped forward with a swish to refill it. Lillie cringed as his cape rattled the delicate snowflake glasses on the sideboard.

"Well," Lillie said softly, "I propose a toast. To the memory of Lady Swindon and the speedy return home of Edgar."

They all held up their glasses.

Lord Swindon swallowed. "I am encouraging Edgar, when this is all over and he is tried and has done his time, to get to know his real father."

Lillie was surprised by this. She had judged Lord Swindon initially as difficult, and stubborn, but he was neither of those things.

"Ireland," Harry mused. "It is a frightfully beautiful place."

"Stunning, yes." Lord Swindon agreed. "And so wild, and *green*—and not just one shade of green. There are olives, and emeralds, and forest greens. Lady Swindon loved it there." He cleared his throat. "Her uncle—Edgar's great uncle—left his Irish estate—Ballyneed, it's called—to her when he died, ten years go. She didn't do much with it, leaving its running to an old caretaker who had been in her uncle's employ for nearly forty years. It's Edgar's estate now. I'll travel there next week and look after it until Edgar is released."

"I'll bet it is quite impressive," Jack said.

"Well, for the most part it is all sheep and craggy rocks and deep lakes. It stretches all the way down to the sea. And the house is an absolutely gorgeous expression of Celtic splendour —but it needs a lot of work. More of it is crumbling than remains upright."

"I think it's nice of you, to put everything that has happened behind you, and move on in a way that is—" Lillie searched carefully for the right words, "well, completely unselfish," she finished.

"I raised him," Lord Swindon answered. "And I love him."

Lillie felt her eyes mist over as she looked around the room and took stock: a Christmas tree that was far too large for its surroundings but erected especially for her, Rumple standing at attention swathed in that ridiculously large holiday cape,

Harry about to wed her dear friend Primrose, her sister, here with her, a cottage awaiting them across the village green, a new job heading up her very own newspaper section, and the love of her life quietly watching her from an overstuffed armchair opposite hers.

Wasn't life, after all the heartache and struggle, still terribly grand?

She quietly gave thanks.

ABOUT THE AUTHOR

Lisa Zumpano is the author of the
LILLIE MEAD HISTORICAL MYSTERY SERIES.
She lives in Vancouver, Canada.

For more information or to join the readers group to be part of
our giveaways, please go to:
www.lisazumpano.com
And receive your free digital copy of